A dee
went

"Honey, do you know what you're doing?" Lyle asked Georgina as her body curved against his, seeking warmth and...

"Please don't talk, she said, curling closer against his strong maleness.

His hand trembled as he stroked her skin, and she let go her tenuous grip on reality, welcoming the tide of feeling. She sent her messages to him silently, as Scott had taught her, waiting for him, wanting him, until she, too, trembled, aching with need.

She whispered his name.

His hands tensed and then pushed her away. "Wake up, Georgina!"

Dazed, she opened her eyes, and he said harshly, "My name is Lyle, not Scott. And I don't need a woman so badly that I'm about to play the part of a dead man."

VANESSA GRANT started writing her first romance at the age of twelve and hasn't forgotten the excitement of having a love story come to life on paper. Currently she teaches business at a community college, but she and her husband are refitting the forty-six-foot yacht they live on with their sons for a world cruise some time in the future. Vanessa believes in love. "After all," she confides, "the most exciting love story I know of is my own."

Books by Vanessa Grant

HARLEQUIN PRESENTS
 895—STORM
1088—JENNY'S TURN

HARLEQUIN ROMANCE
2888—THE CHAUVINIST

Don't miss any of our special offers. Write to us at the following address for information on our newest releases.

Harlequin Reader Service
901 Fuhrmann Blvd., P.O. Box 1397, Buffalo, NY 14240
Canadian address: P.O. Box 603,
Fort Erie, Ont. L2A 5X3

VANESSA GRANT

stray lady

Harlequin Books

TORONTO • NEW YORK • LONDON
AMSTERDAM • PARIS • SYDNEY • HAMBURG
STOCKHOLM • ATHENS • TOKYO • MILAN

Harlequin Presents first edition October 1988
ISBN 0-373-11112-6

Original hardcover edition published in 1987
by Mills & Boon Limited

CHAPTER ONE

INSIDE, there was music, guitar sounds wafting from the large speakers, accompanied occasionally by the sound of percussion instruments.

The house shuddered in the storm, but the sounds of wind and rain were muted. The room was sound-proofed. Carpeted walls and floor. Acoustic tiles on the ceiling. Windows blanketed.

Lyle was bent over the keyboard of the synthesiser, mentally matching words to the music.

His reddish-blond hair kept falling across his forehead. Too many weeks away from a haircut. He pushed it back with a callused hand.

He struck out a word with red ink, wondering where his best pen had disappeared to.

'Daddy?'

'Hmm?' The music flowed, beat a rhythm that told a tale of love and loss. He knew it was good, but the words——

'It's time, Daddy. It's twenty to seven. Time to get the weather.'

'All right. I'm coming.'

'Can I turn off the sinsiser?'

He nodded, watched his young daughter stand up, and two sleeping cats fall, scrambling, to the floor.

She moved across the room to the power switch, one leg slower and weaker than the other. Scruff, the be-draggled mongrel that was the latest addition to their household, trailed at her heels.

She's nothing like Hazel, he thought fleetingly, and was relieved.

7

He crumpled the paper in his fist, then his fingers slipped under Scruff's collar, holding the dog so Robin wouldn't be tripped by clumsy canine feet.

Outside, the dog promptly dived under the engine-room stairs, where it was warm and dry. Lyle and Robin, heads bowed and water streaming off their sou'westers, moved to the high platform that was used to land supplies from the coastguard ships.

'Overcast,' decided Robin, squinting up at the sky. The sun would be setting soon, but already the sky had darkened with the storm.

'What about the sea?' Lyle asked absently, his own eyes intent on something he thought he'd seen in the fog.

'Rough.'

The foghorn blared behind them.

Could it be a sail?

His heart slammed against his ribs, his body tensing at a sudden surge of adrenalin. My God! A sail! In this weather!

'Daddy! You're hurting my hand!'

'Sorry, honey.'

It was gone now. No boat. No sail. Only the drifting fog and driving rain.

You could see anything in the fog if you looked hard enough. It drifted and twisted. Shapes came flowing out of a man's mind to take form in the mist.

Ghostly nightmares, like an impossibly frightening vision of Hazel returning to take Robin away from him.

It had been nothing, just the top of a breaking wave.

Heaven knew, he'd seen enough maniacs heading north for Alaska, but surely not in the midst of a March gale?

'All right, Robin. Let's get out of this stuff.'

Her hand was cool. He slipped his arm around her waist and they ran together, laughing, into the basement.

Scruff didn't come.

'Get out of those wet things, honey. Are you cold? No? Well, I am. We'll have hot chocolate with our strawberries tonight. Why don't you go up and put a kettle on the stove.'

Could it have been a boat out there?

Worried, he went back outside, but there was nothing. Just the lighthouse and the fog.

'Good evening, the lighthouses. This is Prince Rupert Coastguard Radio for the local weather reports.'

He heard Murray's voice sputtering on the radio as he came back inside. The voice sounded as if it belonged to a tall, thin, pipe-smoking Englishman, although Murray was short, round and prematurely bald.

Robin returned in pyjamas and dressing-gown, just as Lyle got to the microphone. She sat cross-legged on the floor as Murray started his collection of local weather reports.

'Green Island?'

Lyle picked up the big microphone. 'Good evening, Murray. We're overcast. Visibility one half-mile in rain and fog. Winds south-east four-five and gusting. Sea rough, with a moderate westerly swell.'

'Roger, Lyle. Stand by for traffic after the local weathers.'

'Standing by.'

They waited while the other lighthouses gave their weathers, then Lyle wrote down the message.

'It's a deadhead,' Murray said, indicating that the message was an unofficial one, probably telephoned in to the coast station. 'It's addressed to your brother. The message reads: "I'm in hospital, but don't worry. It was a false alarm. Baby and I are waiting for you. Love, Dorothy."'

'Thanks, Murray. I'll relay it to Russ.'

So his sister-in-law was in hospital now, waiting for the baby to come. Knowing that, Russ would be more impatient than ever, worrying helplessly, while he was stuck on a lighthouse island forty miles away from her.

There was no hurry to deliver the message. Russ would be sleeping, resting in preparation for the night shift. Lyle went upstairs to his nightly snack with Robin.

Upstairs, Robin spilled her strawberries all over the kitchen floor. Tom, the orange cat, prowled around, sniffing and licking at the stickiness. Dixie, half-Siamese and too lazy to stir, slept on the warming tray over the stove.

Robin watched Tom licking strawberries.

'The floor's clean——' she began.

'No!' he said firmly, rejecting a vision of Robin and the cat licking up the berries together. 'You can eat mine. I'm not very hungry, anyway.' He pushed the cat aside and started cleaning up the mess.

Later, he'd make himself a sandwich.

Robin got ready for bed, then took her time looking for a music tape to play in her Walkman. She hovered over a Bryan Adams tape, then chose one that Lyle had recorded for her.

In her room, he pulled the covers up high around her shoulders, kissing her as she wound her thin arms around his neck.

'You've got your radio?' he asked.

She nodded. The two-way radio was on her bedside table. Lyle turned it on and adjusted the volume.

'Are you going outside, Daddy?'

'For a bit. I'm going over to deliver Russ his message. I'll have a radio with me. Just call if you need me.'

'Be sure 'n wear your jacket. 's cold outside.'

'I will.' She pulled the headphones on and he kissed her again, before he left her listening to the unpublished sounds of Lyle Stevens's music.

She should have a mother, he thought, as he glanced back at her.

And he should have a wife.

But not another Hazel.

Dixie, the Siamese, had finally come down from the stove and was checking out the floor. She managed to find a spot of strawberry juice that Lyle had missed. He wiped up the floor again, then washed their dishes.

He checked Robin once more before he went out. She was already asleep.

He opened the door to let the cats out. Tom started out, then changed his mind. Dixie took one look at the rain outside and headed back for the kitchen stove.

Lyle went out alone.

Russ's windows were dark. Lyle took the stairs two at a time, then worked his way through the storm doors into the kitchen. There were no lights, no sound at all except the howling wind outside. He turned on the kitchen light, grimaced at the pile of dirty dishes that Russ seemed to be saving for Dorothy's return. Lyle had shared a room with Russ when they were boys. As far as he could see, his brother hadn't changed his house-keeping habits at all in the intervening years. If anything, he might be worse.

He shrugged and taped the note to the refrigerator. If Russ didn't find it there when he woke up, he would see it written in the radio log when he went over to give the early morning weather report at four-thirty.

The rubber rain-jacket squeaked as Lyle moved. He switched off the light, closing the doors carefully against the wind.

Scruff came dashing up the stairs to meet him. Lyle grabbed the rail to keep his balance as the dog hurled himself against his legs. 'Got tired of hiding under the engine-room, did you? Take it easy, Scruff. We'll get inside, out of this storm.'

The dog ran off towards the boardwalk, then came tearing back with a whimper.

Lyle scratched at his ear as he came close. 'Restless, are you? Let's go for a walk, then.'

The dog wasn't the only restless one. How many times would he look out over the wild North Pacific waters tonight before he could get rid of the feeling that something was wrong?

The sun had set, leaving just enough daylight to see the strange calm of the water to the north of the island. Small though Green Island was, it made an effective barrier to the wind, creating a broad stretch of almost flat water in its lee.

At the far end of the island, Scruff went tearing over the rocks, whimpering. He stopped suddenly, standing dead still, staring out over the water to the north, shivering.

What had he seen?

Lyle started to follow, stumbled on the dark rocks and stopped. He waited for the lighthouse light to illuminate the rocks ahead.

Scruff whimpered again and looked back at his master.

'I don't know what you're trying to tell me, Scruff.' Lyle hoped his voice would calm the dog, but the eerie violence of the night was affecting both dog and master.

Scruff yelped, a sharp bark, then ran swiftly along the edge of the rocks.

Lyle found himself searching the water again, finding nothing.

'Nothing there. Come on! Let's go home.'

Scruff followed after a moment, still whimpering. When they arrived at the house the dog stopped, hung his head and began whimpering again.

What now? Forcibly haul him into the house? Then put up with this whining and yelping for the next few hours?

Leave him outside in the storm?

'Scruff——' he began helplessly.

Scruff threw back his head and emitted a long, mournful howl.

'Oh, all right! I'm probably crazy, but I feel a bit the same way myself. Just give me a minute to check on Robin, then we'll take another look.'

Robin was sleeping with the headphones askew on her tousled hair. Lyle carefully lifted them away and traced the wires until he found the Walkman tangled in her blankets.

He closed Robin's door carefully. Then he went into the porch and got out his wide-angle binoculars and a powerful portable spotlight.

Scruff was lying under the stairs, staring up, waiting for Lyle. He shuffled to his oversized feet as his master came down the stairs.

As if the dog could understand, Lyle said, 'Don't expect much. We've probably both got island fever. There's nothing but waves and floating logs out there. You just stay put under the stairs. I'm going up the light tower.'

At the top of the tower, the powerful white light rotated night and day, marking Green Island's position on the inland shipping lane, sending its message to mariners... 'Danger, rocks, keep clear'. The light was surrounded by glass panels. Outside the glass, a walkway provided the best look-out position on the island. On warm, sunny days this was an inviting place for seeing the world, the beautiful blue expanse that swept from the southern extreme of Chatham Sound to the Alaska Panhandle. Tonight it was a cold, miserable outlook. Lyle climbed the circular lighthouse stairs, stopped to tie his sou'wester so the wind wouldn't tear it off, and emerged outside.

He searched the water with the powerful binoculars, following the sweeping beam of the white light behind him. The darkness was deepening by the moment. He tried to focus on the dark shadow of Grey Islet to the north.

A strange shape protruded up from the rocks, glistening white in the beam from the light tower.

He waited endless seconds until the light swept over Grey Islet again. His heart was pounding with an ominous conviction.

It wasn't a log. Could it be a sail? Earlier, he could have sworn he had seen a sail.

He turned his binoculars on to the water between the two islands, searched wave tops and troughs in the sweeping white light.

Nothing.

Scruff was waiting at the door to the light tower. He followed behind Lyle, silent but unnaturally tense. Animals sensed things that people were blind to. Not that Scruff was a Lassie, but——

'I'm probably going insane. They say lightkeepers are odd, and I'm about to prove it.' He pushed his hair back absently and opened the basement door.

The dog followed him to the radio-room.

'Prince Rupert Coastguard Radio, this is Green Island.'

Almost immediately, Murray's voice answered.

'Green, Prince Rupert. Go ahead, Lyle.'

'Murray, have you got any boats in trouble? Overdue vessels?'

Static crackled over the speaker as Lyle waited. Scruff leaned against his chair and Lyle scratched him behind the ear.

'Green, Prince Rupert... Nothing much, Lyle. A fishing-boat broken down in the Hecate Strait. He's OK, though. There's a fish packer in the area that's just taking him in tow now. Have you got something there?'

Lyle grimaced at the microphone. 'Maybe just my imagination. There's something over on Grey Islet, but I'm not positive it's not a big log. I'll go take another look.'

'OK, Lyle. I'll query Rescue Co-ordination Centre, but I imagine if they had anything in this area, we'd know about it.'

'Thanks, Murray. I'll get back to you.'

Feeling foolish, Lyle exchanged his rain-jacket for a buoyant floater jacket. He had no real intention of going into the water, but if he suddenly found he had to, he didn't want to have to waste time returning to the house for the proper gear.

Scruff followed Lyle up the stairs to Russ's house. Lyle didn't bother to try to keep Scruff outside. Russ had such a mess inside, one dog wouldn't make much difference to it.

'Russ, get up and give me a hand!'

Russ was sprawled over the bed, thoroughly tangled in a sheet, with the blankets half dragging on to the floor. He rolled over and pushed his face into the pillow as Lyle walked into the bedroom.

'Come on! I need some help outside. I think there might be a boat wrecked on Grey Islet!'

'What?' He was sitting now, coming alert quickly. 'A wreck?' He took his trousers from Lyle's hands and started dressing. 'What kind of a boat? How many people on board?'

'I'm not even sure there's a boat at all, but I saw something over there. Get your things on and come down to the north end of the island.'

Scruff pushed his nose into Russ's lap and earned a hefty shove from Russ's muscled hand. 'Get out of here, you mongrel,' muttered Russ without any heat.

The wind had shifted to beat on Lyle's back as he walked down the boardwalk with Scruff. Once he was on the helicopter pad, he used the flashlight beam to find his way over the rocks. He didn't use the spotlight. Not yet.

He stopped at the water's edge, looking down to where the water moved sluggishly, angrily, in the lee of the island. He switched the brilliant spotlight on, lifting it, trying to settle the beam above the water, on to the rocks of Grey Islet.

'Looks like part of a sail,' said Russ as he came up behind Lyle.

'That's what I thought. Hold the spot, will you? I want to try the binoculars. I tried earlier in the beam of the tower light, but it sweeps too fast for a good look.'

Russ braced himself sturdily against the wind and held the spotlight fairly steady, the beam spreading as it crossed the water to Grey Islet.

'It *is* a sail!' Lyle's voice was thrown away by the wind. 'A mast, broken on the rocks, and what looks like the bow section of a boat. It's smashed to bits—a real mess!'

Russ lowered the light. 'If anybody was on it—in this storm, any loose wreckage—any bodies—would be blown north.'

North. Deep water. No towns. No villages. No islands until the Alaska Panhandle.

Lyle turned away from the water. 'I'm going to launch the inflatable and take a look out there.'

'In the dark? In this storm? You can't go out there!'

'I'll tie a rope on, and leave one end on shore here in case I can't get back under my own power.'

Russ followed across the rocks, and grasped Lyle's muscular arm with his own hard hand. 'You're crazy, Lyle! You'll see as much from shore here as you could——'

'Maybe.' Lyle ignored the attempt at restraint, but his arm was free and he was walking swiftly, throwing back, 'Get the polyprop rope from the engine-room, will you? I'll bring the inflatable down.'

Six hundred feet of rope. Lyle knew it wouldn't let him get even half-way to Grey Islet, but he had to get out there on the water. Why, he wasn't sure.

He took a minute to return to the radio, to tell Murray, 'I've spotted wreckage of a sail-boat on Grey Islet. We're still looking for signs of survivors.'

Murray's response was the practised calm of a man accustomed to emergencies. 'I'll notify RCC. We'll put out a request for mariners to come to your assistance. Can you get over there?'

'Not in this storm. I'm going to look around the calm area, in the lee of the island, but that's all I can do.'

Murray's voice was ringing out over the international distress frequency on Lyle's marine VHF radio upstairs, as Lyle dragged the inflatable out of the basement and threw it into the trailer behind a small tractor.

'... Relay. Mayday Relay. Mayday Relay. An unknown sailing vessel is reported wrecked on Grey Islet, one mile north of Green Island Lighthouse. Mariners in the area are requested to...'

Lyle doubted if many other mariners were foolish enough to be out in this storm. Certainly most of the fishermen knew better. The fool at the helm of this sail-boat obviously hadn't had the sense to stay safely in harbour until the storm abated.

The fishermen and tug-boat crews knew the dangers, but Lyle had seen too many ill-prepared pleasure-boats setting sail for Alaska as if it were a weekend picnic.

The roar of the tractor's engine was swallowed by the wind. He had to drive slowly on the boardwalk. The wind was catching at the bulk of the tractor and trailer, threatening to push him off the boardwalk on to the rocky beach below.

They fastened the rope to a surveyor's tripod on the shore, then Lyle inflated the dinghy and climbed into it.

Within moments he found a floating orange life-belt. He hooked it with the boat-hook and brought it aboard. The words *Lady Harriet* were painted on the round ring.

He glanced back to shore. Russ, as instructed, was searching the water with the binoculars and spotlight.

Lyle had a smaller spotlight and he was making his own
search from water level.

A plastic dinner plate floating upside down. He didn't
try to retrieve that.

Surprising that any of the wreckage had floated this
way, with the wind so strong from the south. It must be
some combination of tidal current and back eddies from
the wind as it bent around the islands.

His radio crackled urgently. Lyle pulled the portable
off his belt, holding it close to his face.

'Go ahead, Russ!'

'Something yellow in the water to your right!'

Lyle moved his spotlight, sweeping the wave tops. As
his dinghy rose on the swell, he spotted the reflective
yellow for a second, then lost it again.

Yellow. It was a colour commonly used for life-jackets
and survival gear.

It took a long time to get the dinghy over to the floating
yellow. The rope was dragging back, pulling against him,
making the rowing difficult. He considered untying the
rope, but decided against it. Even in the shelter of the
island, the water was getting wilder. A fourteen-foot inflatable was no vessel to take on the high seas in a gale.

The body was floating face up, sprawled in the water,
wearing the anti-exposure flotation coveralls that had
become popular among the fishermen in recent years.

Lyle thrust hard with the paddles. The rope pulled
tight. He tried to reach the yellow sailor with the boat-
hook, but missed by several feet.

'Russ, give me more rope!'

'Hold on!' cracked the radio. 'Don't pull on it for a
minute!'

Lyle sat helpless in the dinghy as he drifted farther
away from the floating yellow body.

'OK, go ahead, but for God's sake, don't pull too
hard! I've got it wrapped around a log! I think it'll hold!'

The wind was against him now, swirling up in a back eddy, pushing the dinghy away from the yellow body. Despite Russ's warning, Lyle pushed hard with the oars, swift, powerful strokes that drove him closer. He still couldn't quite get there, but—— He timed his strokes carefully, getting the dinghy surging forward, dropping the paddle and swinging the boat-hook out over the body.

The water surged unexpectedly. The boat-hook swung frighteningly close to the floating man's head. Then, for a miraculous second, everything seemed calm and still. Lyle slipped the hook across the middle of the suit, managing to catch it in the belt.

He pulled slowly on the hook, not wanting to destabilise the floating body. God knew, it didn't look alive, but if he pulled too hard it might turn face down. Those cruiser suits were comfortable, warm, and they floated—but they did nothing to keep an unconscious person's head out of water.

The body swung against the side of the inflatable, dislodging an oar, which promptly drifted away.

The radio crackled. Lyle couldn't spare a hand for it, so he ignored it. He had to get a better grip. He reached over the back of the suit, managed to close his numbing fingers over the belt. Thankfully, those belts were designed for this sort of thing. The tough nylon webbing would hold.

With one hand on the belt, the other slipped under the inanimate arm, he leaned back and pulled hard.

At first nothing happened, then the suit started to slide over the edge of the dinghy. As it came free of the water, he was suddenly pulling too hard. The body was pushing him, throwing him on to the floor of the dinghy.

He landed, gasping, pinned down by the yellow suit and the body in it. Water poured out of the suit, drenching the parts of him that weren't already wet.

He closed his eyes for a second, taking a breath for strength, getting ready to push the man off him and try to start some form of artificial respiration.

Then he felt the warm breath on his face.

The body was alive, but the skin deathly cold.

Hypothermia. In these waters, a man without protection could die of the cold in less than twenty minutes.

But this was no man.

The face was fine-boned, heart-shaped, the long lashes fanning out over pale cheeks, full lips blue with the cold.

Was the cold numbing his brain, creating delusions?

No. It *was* the same woman he'd seen last year, her lively face now pale and lifeless.

He turned to lift the radio, to tell Russ he'd lost an oar and ask to be pulled in. Then he realised that Russ had been watching, was already using the rope to pull the inflatable back towards shore.

Lyle bent close to the face of the woman in his arms, checking again that she was still breathing.

She'd been staying at the Holiday Inn last year. Lyle had been there too, on the same floor, staying at the hotel and visiting Robin twice daily in the nearby Vancouver General Hospital.

A small blonde woman, perhaps in her late twenties, full of lively energy and confidence, with a hint of the vulnerability he'd sensed behind the smiles and the laughter.

She'd had one white streak of hair at her temple. He'd pondered that lock of white hair interrupting the blonde. It had the stylish look of a hairdresser's salon, yet he couldn't see those lively blue eyes belonging to a woman who needed the vanity of an artificial-dye job.

They'd passed in the hallways. He'd said hello and she'd responded. Friendly enough, but her eyes and her voice had acknowledged his attraction to her and rejected it.

A brief fantasy. Ships that had passed in the night. He'd laughed at himself then, for dreaming dreams and thinking in clichés. The reality had been Lyle and Robin returning to this lighthouse haven, Robin recovering from yet another surgical invasion on her body.

The reality had been Cynthia McLeod, a rather futile attempt to find romance where none existed. In some unfortunate way, Cynthia had reminded him too much of Hazel.

Lyle stared down at the unconscious woman.

How had she come to be here, a victim of shipwreck on his island? He'd thought her a restless city girl, far too civilised for the high seas.

The coveralls had protected her, preserved some of her body warmth.

What other injuries? A gash on her face testified that she had been battered against something—a rock, a log? As the lighthouse beam swept over her, Lyle found evidence that more than her face had taken a beating. The suit was torn in several places.

What damage had he done to her, roughly yanking her into the dinghy?

He couldn't tell, but he would have to move her again, to carry her across the rocks, put her into the back of the tractor.

There was a frightening, awkward moment as Lyle passed the unconscious woman to Russ. A wave pulled the dinghy away from shore. Lyle started to lose his balance. Russ caught at the woman and somehow lifted her out of Lyle's arms just in time.

Then he jumped out of the dinghy himself and got her in his arms again, carried her over the rocks and laid her gently down in the trailer.

'I've got to warm her up!' he shouted to his brother as he started the tractor. 'Get word to the coastguard— the boat was the *Lady Harriet*. I found a life-ring—

then see if you can spot any other survivors—oh, but tell the coastguard we need a doctor on the radio!'

If only there were a doctor here!

Don't move an accident victim. Call for the doctor, the ambulance. She might have broken ribs, perhaps internal injuries.

Hypothermia kills. He had to get her warm.

He put her on his bed, stripped off the padded nylon suit and the clothes below, cursing himself for his masculine reaction to her small, beautifully formed body, the unexpectedly full thrust of her naked breasts, the woman's curve of her hip and buttocks.

He found his fingers lingering on the full curve of her torso, the thrust of her hip.

Stop fantasising!

He took his hands away from her body, but couldn't stop his mind. From the first time he'd seen her, he'd been able to imagine this woman in his arms, their bodies twisted together in a dance of love. She'd be warm, passionate. Right now she was motionless as death, but he knew she was a warm, passionate, loving kind of woman.

A woman who belonged to another man.

On her left hand she wore a broad gold wedding band.

He should have expected that. How could a woman like this be free, not claimed by some lucky man? He wouldn't be the only man who had felt this way about her.

Without even knowing her.

Crazy, that's what he was! A crazy lightkeeper.

'Where'd she come from?' whispered a small voice behind him as he lowered the unconscious woman into the warm water of the bathtub.

'The water,' he answered absently.

'How'd she get in the water?' He glanced up and found Robin standing beside him, idly rubbing her weak leg with the palm of her hand.

'Her boat smashed on Grey Islet.'

'There's blood on her. Is she dead?'

'No... No!'

She must have been swept up against the rocks at one point. Her leg had a deep gash that was starting to bleed in the warm water. There was a big scrape on her side that might mean broken ribs, and a cut on her face that would be painful healing.

If only she would open her eyes!

CHAPTER TWO

THE warmth came slowly, like pain returning with wakefulness. With the warmth came the dreams. George shifted, rolling, trying to escape the voices that echoed both inside and outside the dream.

Scott's voice, firm and sure and loving.

No, that was wrong. Not Scott. She'd been sailing, hadn't she? Alone?

Collections of odd words isolated from reality.

'. . . issued a notice to mariners, but with the storm and the dark . . . gale warning, building to a storm. No let-up . . .'

'. . . no identification on her. No idea . . . must have been others on board . . . still unconscious . . . hypothermia and lord knows what else! . . . don't think any actual broken bones, unless the ribs . . . .'

'. . . vital signs . . . breathing better . . .'

Men's voices. Who were they talking about? Her?

No, she was dreaming. She had been sailing, but she was at anchor now, dreaming the voices.

She felt the water surging under *Lady Harriet*, sweeping her away from the pain.

Today . . . Funny, mixing up the days. Today was . . .

Prince Rupert this morning. A fisherman warning her, 'Storm coming. South-easter.'

She'd laughed, shaking her short blonde curls. 'There's no storm forecast.'

'Gales in Chatham Sound before night,' he'd insisted.

She hadn't told him that she didn't really care if there was a gale.

24

A ferry had passed her in the harbour entrance. Someone on the bridge had looked down at her small sail-boat, hailing her with a friendly greeting.

'You're looking pretty down there, *Lady Harriet*!'

The ferry had turned south. George had sailed her little ship off to the north once she was clear of the dangers.

It had been one of the better days, with the sun high in a cloudy sky and the water blue and exciting. Scott's memory had been a gentle sadness, not paining her.

Sailing alone was hard work; it had kept her from thinking.

When the wind had freshened and the clouds drew together, she'd scrambled out on deck to take down the Genoa, putting up a smaller sail in its place, hanging on desperately as the deck heaved violently underfoot.

She'd crawled back to the cockpit, scared, but feeling a wild surge of triumph that she'd managed a difficult job alone.

When the wind had picked up even more she was singing, riding wild, north to Alaska...

'Wake up! Hey, sweetheart, you must wake...have to know about...'

The pain surged back, covering her until she could hardly hear the voice trying to pull her back. Not Scott's voice.

Silence.

She rested, letting her body sag against the mattress. In her mind, she heard music. She let the hurt seep away, drifting until the bright light penetrated her eyelids.

She moved her head, trying to escape the brilliance. Waves of pain from her chest shocked her into immobility.

Something on her head. She lifted a weak hand, felt some barrier of metal.

Hands on her hair.

She opened her eyes, saw headphones in small hands. A light voice whispered, 'You're 'wake now?'

A small girl, long blonde hair floating around her shoulders, pale blue eyes staring.

A dream?

Where was this?

...sailing, riding the waves as the wind freshened to a storm, then...

'Did you like the music?'

'Music?' She focused on the girl. How old? Nine? Ten?

'It's my Walkman.' She held a tape player cradled carefully in her hands. 'I like the music when I don' feel good.'

Talking seemed so complicated. She nodded. Her face hurt.

Where was she? *Lady Harriet?*

The girl bounced slightly on the bed. George tried not to wince at the motion.

'What's your name? I'm Robin.'

What had happened to her? She felt as if she'd fallen down a flight of stairs.

'Your name?' asked the girl again.

'George.' Her tongue was swollen, her throat scratchy.

'That's a boy's name.'

George smiled and found that even her lips hurt.

When she closed her eyes, the pain receded.

The next time she opened her eyes, the light from the ceiling seemed dimmer. The little girl was gone. In her place, two men were standing at the foot of her bed. They were both fair and broad, both wearing orange Mustang jackets, and both staring down at her.

She tried to resolve the image into something that made sense.

'Delirious,' she muttered.

It was all dreams...*Lady Harriet*...the girl...the music. She'd wake up soon. Scott would be there.

'Wake up... George, wake up!'

Hands on her shoulders, a rough gentleness. The voice from the dream. She rolled her head in protest, but the voice went on.

'Wake up!'

'I'm dizzy,' she croaked. 'There's two of you.'

The voice laughed, a pleasing, husky rumble. Something familiar about that voice. Oh, yes. The dream.

'There really are two of us, George. Is your name really George? You've got to answer some questions.'

She didn't have any answers. Just keep moving, keep running, so it doesn't catch up with you.

She drifted on a tide of dizziness, escaping the insistent voice, going back to Scott, back to the good times.

Lady Harriet.

Scott.

They'd found the boat tied to a float in Alaska, a *For Sale* sign pasted in her window.

They were on holiday, enjoying new sights, Scott tolerantly letting George speculate on everything they saw... should they buy a house here and move north to Alaska?... no, perhaps not, but what about another holiday in Alaska next year? Or perhaps...

George came to an abrupt stop in front of a thirty-foot sail-boat, her arm jerking tight as Scott walked on, still holding her hand.

'Scott, isn't it beautiful? And it's for sale.'

He'd laughed down at her, his warm, brown eyes not taking her seriously.

'Georgina, I don't think——'

'Scott, think what fun it was sailing in Tahiti! It doesn't hurt to look.'

They had looked. Why had Scott decided to offer for the boat? Had he caught her enthusiasm? Or was it just another of the things he had done for love of her?

A new coat of paint. Plans and charts and sailing guides.

Their sailing trip. A dream trip.

Scott arranging to hand over most of his work to his partner, take a couple of years for their cruise.

Dreams...

'How many on board?' the voice was demanding, intruding. Scott dissolved and there was only the question. 'How many?'

She opened her eyes, stared up at the face bent over hers. Reddish hair in a tousled disarray, deep blue eyes blazing down into hers. Her eyes got caught in a hypnotic tracing of the deep lines of his face.

'On board?' she repeated stupidly.

His voice lowered, as he said slowly, 'You were on a boat. *Lady Harriet*. You remember that, don't you?' She nodded. 'Who else was on the boat with you?'

He looked like a determined man. Stubborn. Tough. With dreamer's eyes.

She smiled, wondering which had the upper hand—the dreamer in his eyes? Or the tough realist?

'Don't go back to sleep! Come on! Open your eyes. Look at me.'

'You need a haircut,' she mumbled.

His eyes had changed. Harder. More determined.

'Tired,' she muttered heavily.

She stared at his lips as they moved in meaningless speech. '...how many people were aboard that boat?'

Jenny last year...Scott...Scott standing behind her, arms around her, helping her steer...kissing the back of her neck. Scott setting the anchor, taking her hand and leading her down below, to their state-room with the big double berth.

'How many?'

She shook her head, blinking helplessly as tears filled her eyes. The dreamer-man's hands came to her shoulders, shaking her gently.

'Who was aboard? You and your husband? Anyone else?'

Her husband! Scott...

If the crying started, it might never stop.

'Just me,' she whispered, then she caught at the drifting darkness and escaped his questions.

It was night when she drifted back to consciousness.

Quiet.

She opened her eyes. A darkened room, lit up every few seconds by the sweep of a light. She was in a bed, not in *Lady Harriet*'s bunk. A thick quilt was pulled up around her shoulders.

The room was sparsely furnished, as if it were seldom used. Beside the bed was a big chair—too big for the room. A man was sleeping in it. The man from her dreams.

His eyes opened as she watched.

'Awake?' His voice was deep and soft, then sharper, 'No, don't try to move too quickly! You're hurt.'

The pain rushed over her as she tried to sit, then slowly receded. 'I've broken a rib,' she whispered at last.

The water. *Lady Harriet* wrecked on the rocks. She felt pain, as if she were losing Scott all over again. She pushed the memories away.

'I wouldn't be surprised,' he said, 'but it'll be all right if you lie still.'

He bent over her and pulled the quilt back up to her neck. She felt the warm brush of his hand against her cheek. 'Just take it easy. The doctor says you shouldn't try to move much for a couple of days.'

'Doctor?'

She'd been far from anywhere, sailing hard and fast. No doctors. No hospitals. Her eyes searched quickly around the room as the light swept past again.

'Remote-control doctor.' His voice was very pleasing, reassuring, reflecting the warmth she felt from his eyes. 'You're on Green Island Light Station. We found you in the water yesterday evening, after your ship was wrecked. We had the doctor on the radio. He says you sound all right.'

The smile was in his voice and she found herself smiling back, ignoring the pain from cracked lips.

'I'm the doctor's eyes and hands, and he doesn't think there's anything wrong that won't heal. How do you feel?'

Eyes. And hands. Had she dreamed hands on her bare skin, warm and gentle, yet rough with a man's hard-skinned toughness?

'How do you feel? Any sharp pains?' He brushed hair away from her forehead.

'No,' she whispered, oddly self-conscious of his eyes on her face. Her skin felt stiff, like fragile paper.

'Does it hurt to breathe?' He gestured vaguely towards her chest.

He'd pulled her out of the water. The dreams had been real. His hands had probed her naked body to assess the damage done by her spill in the ocean. She dropped her eyes to her own hands, lying clenched on the bedclothes.

Of course it didn't matter that he'd undressed her. She had pains all over, as if she'd been battered on the rocks. He'd been right to check her carefully for injuries.

She cleared her throat, forcing herself to ignore the rawness that must have come from the salt water.

'A lighthouse?' She could feel the rushing water, the noise of the storm. Her memories made the silence seem unreal.

He was unreal too, with his gentle, dreaming eyes and his hard, callused hands.

'Yes. Green Island. We—my brother and I—found you in the water. Do you remember what happened?'

Wild water, racing out of control. George shook her head. She didn't want to remember.

'I'm sorry—I have to make sure. There was no one else on board?'

'Just me.' She managed a laugh, until the pain in her chest stopped the laughter, but she was still smiling, saying, 'You don't believe a woman could go sailing alone?'

It seemed oddly important that he should realise she was capable of single-handing her boat, that she didn't need anyone else.

He shrugged, seemed strangely uncomfortable. 'You're so small, and it's heavy work pulling on sails, even though you're quite well muscled.'

Her face flamed as his eyes moved over the blankets that covered her, as if he were remembering how her body had looked.

'You're wearing a wedding ring. Where's your husband?'

She felt the familiar tide of loss welling up inside, pushed herself up to a half-sitting position, wincing, welcoming the pain that momentarily overwhelmed thoughts of Scott.

'Hey, take it easy!' His strong arms were behind her, taking the weight of her as she started to collapse back against the bed. 'Don't move too fast—let things heal!'

'I'm all right,' insisted George, but she found herself resting against his strong arm, letting him settle her back down without protest.

'You will be,' he agreed softly, 'but give it time. Let me look after you.'

Scott had looked after her, kept her out of trouble. She smiled, letting her eyes close.

Then that soft voice shattered her smile. 'If you give me your husband's name and address, I can arrange for him to get word that you're all right. Or—if there's someone else I should contact?'

She wanted to drift away again, but he was going to come after her, drag her back with hurtful questions.

She squeezed her eyes shut as she said the words. 'He's dead.'

Lyle was silent a moment, watching her, forcing himself not to show the primitive surge of relief he felt at learning that she did not belong to another man after all.

The sea brought her, and she's mine.

'Who should we notify, then? Someone must be expecting you.'

Her eyes opened. She shook her head.

'Your family?' he persisted.

He welcomed the laughter that suddenly glinted in her eyes as she whispered, 'They're not expecting me. They're used to this.'

'Used to shipwrecks?' he asked incredulously, bringing the smile to her lips as well.

'No, I haven't been shipwrecked before.' She cleared her throat. 'Lately I've been away a lot, and I haven't—— Well, I haven't always kept in touch.' She stopped talking. He waited, hoping she would say more.

Talking was getting easier. She said, 'If my mother and Jenny don't hear from me, they'll just decide that I'm off on some crazy adventure. They'd only worry if they knew about this.' She frowned, asked abruptly, '*Lady Harriet*'s gone?'

'Yes,' he agreed casually. She hadn't talked about the wreck, didn't seem to want to talk about it.

He went away, returning almost immediately with a bowl of thick, hot soup. He fed her silently until she turned her head away.

'Would you like anything else? Water? Juice?'

She shook her head.

He was a big man, with big hands that held the empty soup bowl awkwardly. The silence seemed filled with some meaning. She forced her eyes away from his, said nervously, 'When I was sleeping—I thought there was music.'

The smile curved his lips. 'My daughter,' he explained. 'She thought you'd like the music, that it would make you feel better, so she brought her Walkman in here, put the headphones on your ears.'

The girl had been his daughter. So he had a family, a wife and child who received the warmth of that smile, the strength of those arms.

Scott... How terribly she missed Scott! More than ever now, lying alone in a strange house on a strange island.

'You don't need to look after me.' Her voice dropped to a whisper as the hoarseness from the salt water made itself felt. 'Send me into a hospital or something.'

'You're not going anywhere,' he said, a gentle amusement showing in those deep blue eyes. 'There's a storm outside. You couldn't find anyone willing to pilot a plane or a boat out here in this weather.'

'Oh.' Then she smiled wryly, realising, 'No one but me.' She remembered the fisherman who had warned her about the storm.

'Do you want me to send word to your insurance agent? You'll be filing a claim? You were insured, weren't you?'

'Yes.' She had renewed the policy just last month. 'The papers were on *Lady Harriet*.'

'The agent? You know his name?'

George gave him the name. He went off to radio a message that would be relayed to her agent in Victoria.

Strange man. Muscular and—well, sexy—and radiating the confidence of a man who knew how to deal with life and the world.

A lighthouse keeper? He didn't seem a recluse, but he had the eyes of an artist or a dreamer, and the hands of a healer—hard, callused hands that were gentle against the painful spots.

What had brought him here? Green Island. She hadn't seen it in daylight, but on the chart it had been a small blob of land tossed into the north end of Chatham Sound.

What would a man like this want with a life of restricted isolation?

He was evidently a family man, but where was his wife?

He had pulled her out of the water, tended to her needs, removed her clothes. She was dressed in an over-sized man's sweatshirt, and the only female she'd seen any sign of was the small girl with the long, blonde hair.

'I have to get up,' she said uncomfortably as he came back through the door. Crazy! She had just turned thirty, was certainly no young girl, but she didn't know how to tell him that she had to use the bathroom.

'All right,' he agreed easily, pulling back her blankets. 'I don't think you should walk—I taped up a pretty deep gash on your leg. I wouldn't want you walking on it yet.'

He lifted her easily in strong arms. He carried her into the bathroom and stood her carefully on her feet.

'Hang on, will you? Don't put your weight on that leg. There's a new toothbrush in the medicine cabinet. You can use that, and make yourself at home.'

Her eyes went longingly to the bathtub, but Lyle said quickly, 'Better wait for that. I wouldn't want that cut opening up again.'

He left her alone, closing the door carefully behind him, giving her the privacy she needed.

She brushed her teeth, wishing she could close her eyes and make everything disappear. She didn't want to be stranded here on an island with a man who asked too many questions, even if his eyes were warm and his hands gentle. She should be on her way, out of here.

Oh, God! She had to get moving again, and quickly, or it was all going to catch up with her. Scott. And now *Lady Harriet*.

When she got back into the bed, she somehow managed to go back to sleep, keeping her brain numb enough so that none of the memories came to haunt her.

The next time she woke, her eyes fixed on a tall man at the foot of her bed.

'I'm Russ.' He identified himself with a self-conscious grin. 'Just checking on you. Are you all right?'

For just a second she had thought it was the man with the dreamer eyes. 'Your brother?' she asked slowly.

'Lyle, that's my brother.' He grinned. 'Earlier you thought you were seeing double, but there really are two of us.'

Lyle. He'd been good to her in the night. His brother was younger, a little less certain of himself. She asked, 'Are there more of you? You and Lyle and a little girl?'

'Robin. That's Lyle's daughter. There's my wife, Dorothy, but she's away right now. Do you want anything? Food? A drink? Lyle's sleeping, so I'm on shift right now.'

'No, thanks.' She closed her eyes, then murmured, 'And thanks for rescuing me.'

'Thank Lyle for that. All I did was stand on shore and watch.'

What about Lyle's wife? Why hadn't Russ mentioned her?

She slept and woke. And slept again.

Whenever she woke, she found someone watching over her. Lyle. Robin. Occasionally Russ. Once she opened her eyes, saw Lyle watching her, and knew that he thought her a very desirable woman.

Three years alone must have left her unusually aware of the hard-muscled attractiveness of a personable man, because she had to stop her eyes from answering his.

Lyle. A married man with a daughter and a mysteriously absent wife.

She slept. She dreamed that Lyle was holding out his hand to her. She drew back, fearful. Then suddenly it was Scott, not Lyle at all. She reached out her own hand, but he disappeared into the fog before she could touch his fingers.

She woke with her hand clutching at nothing.

Robin was there, sitting in the big chair by the bed.

Her eyes were a paler edition of her father's. Her hair was blonde without the red.

'It's my recess time,' she told George as she tucked her legs up. 'I was doing my 'rithmatic.' She looked around the room, as she said offhandedly, 'I could work in here.'

George was awake more often now, sometimes finding herself alone in the sparsely furnished bedroom.

'I'd like that,' she said, watching the smile transform Robin's serious face. 'Do you do your school by correspondence?'

The long hair swept over Robin's face as she nodded. 'My dad helps me. I help him look after the lighthouse, an' he helps me with my school.'

'And your mother?'

The small face darkened and Robin's smile froze. Her eyelids dropped and she rubbed her right leg with one hand.

'I've got work to do,' she mumbled abruptly, standing quickly and moving away without meeting George's eyes, limping as if her foot had fallen asleep as she sat in the big chair.

Why did tears come to Robin's eyes at the mention of her mother? Why hadn't Lyle mentioned a wife?

'I think it's time I got up,' she told Lyle when he brought her dinner later in the day. 'I can't sit here and be waited on.'

'I don't see why not.' He smiled, but his voice was firm. 'I'd rather you didn't walk on your leg.'

'But I——'

'If that cut opens up, I've really no idea what to do about it.' He put a plate of sandwiches down on the bedside table, spreading his long arms in a helpless gesture.

She eyed him suspiciously. 'I don't believe that. I'm sure you'd think of something to do in any emergency.'

He grinned, admitted, 'Perhaps, but please don't put me to the test. Are you really in such a hurry to get up?'

Yes, she was. She must get up. Get away from here.

Lyle and Robin cared for her with unsettling warmth. She wasn't sure why it bothered her so much. Perhaps because she knew that they had something she was never going to have again. Love. A home.

She met his eyes, couldn't seem to hold strong against their warm determination. 'I—I'd like to go for a walk. I'm not used to being looked after like this.' She shrugged, as she added, 'I'm really not very good at it.'

That made him laugh. 'You'd better practise! Are you a reader? Yes? What kind of books?'

She shrugged, remembering the disastrous attempts Scott had made to pick out books for her. Reading tastes were such an individual thing. 'Mysteries, romances. Anything that makes sense. I like my stories to go from beginning to end. I hate books that don't tell the reader what's going on. And I don't like depressing books.'

'Neither do I,' agreed Lyle. She wondered how he'd managed to have such dark, thick eyebrows when his hair was such a fair blondish-red. The brows flattened as he said, 'I can't imagine what good it does anyone to dwell on the depressing things in life. I'll see what I can find you to read.'

He came back with his arms filled with paperbacks.

She shifted to a sitting position, twisting to look eagerly at the covers as the books tumbled to the bed. 'You've raided a book store!'

'We keep a good stock out here.' He moved some of the paperbacks closer to her, then sat down on the edge of the bed. 'I raided my sister-in-law's shelves for the romances.'

George was sorting through the books enthusiastically. 'Nevil Shute! Oh, this one is a favourite of mine! I haven't read it in years.'

He sorted through the books. 'There are more of his here—I'm sort of a collector of them. Because of the airplanes, I suppose.'

'Airplanes? Do you fly?'

He nodded, smiling. 'I've got a Cessna float-plane. It's in Prince Rupert right now. I'll be bringing it back for the summer when I go out on holidays.'

'You like flying?'

Of course he did. She could see it in his eyes, hear it in his voice as he surprised her by saying, 'I used to fly helicopters commercially.'

'And now——' She was curious and it showed in her voice, but he didn't respond. He found another Nevil Shute and handed it to her. 'Does the plane help to make it less isolated out here?'

'Yes,' he agreed, handing her yet another book.

George shifted in the bed. Some of the books slid off her legs and Lyle rescued them. She stopped more from sliding with a hand, saying eagerly, 'I've always wanted to learn to fly myself. Why did you stop flying commercially? How could you leave flying, to sit on an island in the middle of nowhere?'

'There were reasons.' He stood up, towering over the bed, staring down at her. The smile was gone and his eyes were cold. She wished she hadn't said something to drive away the warmth, but she had, and somehow his memories had hurt him, though he wasn't talking about it. 'Enjoy the books. Just call if you need anything else.'

So he didn't like answering questions about his past. Well, she should understand that. She had enough painful memories of her own.

She picked up a book.

Why had Lyle left a career as a pilot to come out to this place? Had he lost his job?

No. He would be a good pilot, sure and skilful, in-spiring confidence in his passengers.

What about his wife? Had she left him, refusing to live in such isolation? George could understand a woman not wanting to live on a lighthouse. But what about Robin? How could a mother leave her child?

Was she dead?

While she read, a brown and white cat came into the room and up on to the bed, curling itself into a warm ball on George's stomach.

'Are you Dixie?' she asked, scratching under the furry chin.

'Two cats and a dog,' Robin had told her. 'The cats were Tom and Dick, but Dick turned into a girl, so she's Dixie now.'

It was a long time since she'd lounged in bed, reading. It wasn't the same in a hotel, and she'd spent most of her time in hotels since Scott had died.

She hadn't been able to bring herself to sell the house, but she'd rented it out almost immediately. What was the point in staying there, remembering? If there had been a child——

Most mornings Scott had bent to kiss her sleepy face, saying, 'Don't get up, Georgina. You look so contented sleeping there.'

She would twist her arms around his neck and he would murmur, 'Just go back to sleep. Come down to the office later and I'll take you out to lunch.'

When he was gone, she'd stretch out a lazy arm for her book. It had become a habit, a lazy, luxurious habit that went with all the other ways in which Scott had pampered and spoiled her.

She could even remember the name of the book she had been reading that last morning.

Oh, God! Please, no more memories!

She pushed the quilt back with determination, then swung her legs around and slid her bare feet on to the floor.

When she got to her feet, the shirt she was wearing came only to the top of her thighs. She was wearing no panties underneath.

How could she have let Lyle carry her about these last few days, her bare legs drawn up against his chest?

What about her clothes?

She turned towards the empty dresser, lurching as the painful leg refused to support her, then found Robin at her side.

'Are you all right, George?' The girl's pale blue eyes looked up at her, worried. 'I'll help you back to bed.'

'I'm OK, Robin.'

'Do you want me to get my dad?' the girl asked. 'He's over talking to Uncle Russ. I can go and——'

'It's all right.' How could she be so weak that she needed a small child to nurse her? She collapsed back on to the bed.

Robin seemed more than equal to the chore, bringing a hot-water bottle to tuck in beside George, then gently fitting the headphones over her curls. Music seemed to be Robin's idea of a cure-all.

'You're a girl after my own heart,' murmured George as she drifted away to the sounds of a bass guitar. Tomorrow she would get up for sure, she promised herself as she let the sleepiness overtake her. But she didn't.

'Not yet,' said Lyle firmly. What was wrong with her? She didn't even protest his decree.

Robin had brought her schoolwork with her this morning. George helped her with a maths problem, then with a reading assignment, trying to help Robin answer a question on why Porgy was afraid to go down the path beside the old hen house.

'That's all I have to do,' said Robin as she carefully wrote the last few words of her answer. 'I'll put my books away. Daddy and I have a snack this time every day. Are you hungry?'

'A little,' George agreed, mainly to please Robin.

Robin carefully picked the two books up together. 'We've run out of strawberries, so Daddy said we could have some more of the ice-cream.'

'I love ice-cream. I haven't had it in—have you hurt your leg, Robin? You're limping!'

'I always limp.' She clutched the books tightly. 'My leg doesn't work right. I was born with it wrong.'

She was so desperately tense, George wanted to put her arms around her. 'It's only a little limp. Does it hurt?'

Robin shifted the books, her eyes clouded. 'Not now. Just when I go to the doctors. They do things, and sometimes they put me to sleep and cut it open and straighten it up a bit.' She glared down at the leg as if it didn't belong to her. 'Daddy says it will get all better in the end.'

George didn't know what she should say.

'Don't you think it's ugly?' demanded Robin. 'People aren't supposed to limp, you know.'

George said, 'I limp. Do you think it makes me ugly?'

Robin shook her head, the long fine hair swirling around her shoulders. 'You're too pretty to look ugly, even if you limp. And yours will get better.'

George touched the healing abrasion on her face. 'Pretty? With this mess on my face? You're far prettier than I am. You've got beautiful eyes and lovely long hair. And your leg's going to get better, too.'

After a tense, silent moment, Robin whispered, 'Do you really think I'm pretty?'

'Really. Very pretty.'

'My mother didn't think so.' Robin stared down at her own hand as it clenched over her thigh.

George said nothing, waiting.

A dog barked outside. Robin looked up and said tonelessly, 'That's Scruff. He's always barking.'

'Scruff? How did Scruff get his name?'

What had Robin's mother done to her daughter?

'Daddy said we had to name him.' She kept her eyes firmly on the foot of the bed, as she said, 'We got him from a fisherman.' She shifted her gaze to the window, anywhere but at George.

'He was put up for 'doption 'cause he got seasick. The man just called him *dog*, an' he was no sailor. Daddy said we should name him Harry—then we'd have Tom, Dick and Harry. But I said Dick was Dixie, anyway, and we should call him Scruff. 'Cause he is. Daddy says he looks like he just crawled out of a back alley... My mummy ran away because she didn't want to be my mummy any more.'

Robin was staring at her, eyes filled with hurt defiance. George shifted in the bed, pushing herself up on the pillows. 'Robin—honey, I can't—I can't imagine anyone not wanting to be your mummy.'

The girl bit her lip. She was trying hard to keep the tears back, but losing the battle. Her pale blue eyes were filled with moisture, her face rigid with the effort of holding back.

In a moment Robin would draw away and the vulnerability would disappear. George was tempted to let that happen, because sharing Robin's hurt came too close to touching her own loneliness.

Then she found herself reaching out, touching the hands that were clenched together so tightly. Robin's hand jerked away, then her fingers were clutching at George's.

George pulled gently, bringing Robin into her arms. A massive shudder went through the girl. She hurled herself against George's injured ribs and the tears started to flow freely.

George managed to shift herself enough to ease the pain against her ribs without disturbing Robin. If there were any words to say to the crying young girl, she didn't know them. She just held her and let the tears come, taking a strange comfort herself from Robin's warm body in her arms.

When Lyle came into the room, she shook her head silently. He stared down at them for a moment, the young girl curled hard against the woman in the bed, her arms thrown around George's neck. He moved half a step into the room, then stopped.

When he left, she closed her eyes and told herself that her own tears were only for Robin.

It wasn't true. Wherever Robin's mother was, she had left her daughter just as surely as Scott had left George.

CHAPTER THREE

LYING in bed, inactive, it was too easy to start thinking, and George didn't want to think.

It was a relief the day Lyle came to collect her empty breakfast plate and announced, 'I'd like to have another look at that gash on your leg, to be sure it's healing. Then, if the leg looks OK, you could get up.'

His hands were gentle, pressing on the soft skin of her outer thigh. She hoped he didn't realise how oddly his touch made her tremble.

'It looks all right.'

She couldn't see the leg, only Lyle's head, his hair wildly styled by the wind. She'd smelled the tang of the salt air on him when he came into the room.

He put out a hand for balance, his thigh pressing against hers as he probed gently around the bandage. 'Hurt?' he asked suddenly.

She started to shake her head, then yelped as he yanked the tape off in one swift, painful motion. 'Ouch! Yes, that hurts!'

'Sorry. I always hate that part myself, but the tape had to come off.'

'I suppose so,' she admitted unwillingly, her leg still stinging. She felt nervous, too aware of him. 'How does my leg look?' She sat up abruptly, breaking contact with his disturbing blue eyes. 'Can I see?'

'It's healing well—I guess you'll have a scar.'

'I can live with a scar.' She could see gold flecks in the deep blue of his eyes. Feeling the heat from his body, she added nervously, 'It doesn't look as bad as I thought.'

'The scar doesn't bother you?' Could his eyes see things she kept secret even from herself?

'I've been collecting scars all my life,' she said absently. 'I fell out of my first tree when I was five years old.'

'Most of them don't show,' he said gently, as if he could see the scar on her heart. Scott, she thought, and the pain was fresh and strong inside her.

She leaned back against the pillows, but he was still close enough to make her breathless. *Three years*, she thought. Three years of being a woman alone.

Surely he couldn't see the thoughts in her mind? Did he know how conscious she was of him? She dropped her eyes. Perhaps he did. Why else would he look at her like that?

Not long ago, in Mexico, she'd tried to relieve her loneliness with a casual affair, in the mistaken hope that she could diminish the loneliness without intimacy.

The Mexican man had been nice, and attractive. He'd kissed warmly, and it should have been good.

But he wasn't Scott.

George had left Mexico quickly, without explanation, escaping for the solitude of *Lady Harriet*, sailing north too early in the season, riding the spring winds towards Alaska.

Now she was on this rocky island, and it must be her hormones telling her that Lyle could give her the loving she needed.

She knew better. It was Scott she needed. No one else could take that place in her life. She didn't want anyone else.

She broke the long silence abruptly, blinking and tossing her curls back. 'So I can get up? I'd love a shower.'

His eyes dropped to the swelling of her breasts beneath the big sweatshirt, telling her without words that he could visualise her naked under the spray. He looked up, and saw the flush growing on her cheeks.

He knew! Somehow he knew the thoughts she'd been thinking.

He said, 'I think a shower would be all right. Then, afterwards, we'd better bandage the leg again. You won't overdo it, will you?' He stood up, hooked his thumbs in the belt of his jeans, a frown growing on his face. 'I have a feeling you're inclined to throw caution to the winds, and it wouldn't be a good idea with that leg.'

She started to contradict him, but found herself saying instead, 'I won't. At least——'

He covered her lips with light fingers that tingled against her mouth. 'Leave it at that, George. I know you're a wild girl, but be tame for a couple of days, anyway. How are the ribs? OK?'

A wild girl. She winced at that, but it was true. She'd always been the wild one, driving her mother to distraction, worrying Scott. She wouldn't change now, at the age of thirty.

'I'm mending,' she told him. 'I hurt, but I deserve that for going sailing in a storm.'

'I won't argue that.' For a moment she thought he was about to give her a lecture on water safety, then he met her eyes with his own and she saw worry deep beneath the blue.

'George, yesterday, you and Robin—if she tells you anything you feel I should know...'

George smoothed the quilt with her hands. She tried to imagine the woman who was Robin's mother. What had the marriage been like? Had Lyle looked at his wife the way he sometimes looked at her?

Had they slept together in the bed across the hall? George pushed away that strangely disturbing thought, and said, 'Robin told me that her mother left because she didn't want her.' Lyle's hands clenched in an involuntary spasm. She broke out, 'That's a terrible thing for a girl to believe!'

He swung away from her and went to stare out of the window. 'Unfortunately, it's partly true.'

She pushed herself up, her voice rising, 'How could anyone——'

What was it about his eyes? They held none of the overt sexual challenge that she'd learned to ignore in men's eyes, and yet . . .

'How could Robin's mother leave? Because—Robin's such a sweetheart!'

He held out a large bathrobe for her to step into, saying, 'I don't imagine it was all her fault.'

She climbed out of the bed, letting his hands tie the knot at her waist. Against her will, she found herself taking pleasure in the sensation of his hands brushing her midriff through the robe. 'What do you mean?'

'She didn't want motherhood, or marriage, for that matter.' He walked away from her to the window, his voice muffled. 'I suppose they were all my idea, the marriage and the baby and—well, she just reached the point where she couldn't handle it.'

George pulled the robe more tightly around her, frowning, trying to see this nameless woman, trying not to wish his hands had remained at her waist. She couldn't help wondering about the irony of Lyle's wife not wanting children when she, who was childless, had wanted them so badly. 'When—what was her name?'

She hoped he wouldn't answer. His life was coming too close. If she started hurting for Lyle and Robin, the feelings might all come back.

'Hazel,' he said, turning back towards her. She thought he was looking right through her. 'She left five years ago. Robin was three, and she's never talked about it. I haven't asked, because——' He spread his hands, his face showing an uncertain vulnerability. 'I haven't asked, because I didn't want to make her think about it, and also—it wasn't nice.' He laughed bitterly. 'God! That's the understatement of the year! There were fights, and

I would imagine Robin heard at least some of them,
however hard I tried to—well, it seemed better to leave
it and hope it would become part of a forgotten past, a
bad dream.'

George whispered, 'She hasn't forgotten anything. She
thinks the only reason her mother left was to get away
from her, and she thinks it was mainly because of her
leg.'

Lyle replied bitterly, 'Marriage and motherhood were
bad enough from Hazel's point of view, but she didn't
know how to begin to cope with specialists and surgery
and—and a daughter who wasn't physically perfect.
George, I wouldn't know how to start trying to tell Robin
that, and I can't lie to her about it!'

She searched his face.

He had a cheerful mongrel dog that had been cast off
by a fisherman, two cats that had been rescued from the
SPCA, and a daughter unwanted by her mother. As far
as George could see, he loved them all.

She said softly, 'I think Robin will be all right. After
all, she knows you love her... and a girl's father is the
most important thing.'

'I hope so. I—thank you, George.' His hand was so
soft against her face. She found herself turning to rest
her cheek against the callused palm. It was a long
moment before he said softly, 'You'd better get into that
shower before your leg gets too tired. This standing can't
be doing any good.'

He moved to let her pass. As she was going through
the doorway to the bathroom he asked softly, 'What
about your marriage, George?'

Why had she let this happen? Couldn't they just be
strangers, with secret lives?

'I loved him,' she whispered. 'We were very happy.'

He said nothing. She added, 'We were married for
nine years. He died three years ago.'

'And you haven't stopped missing him?'

'I'll never stop missing him,' she said flatly, limping away from him and closing herself into the bathroom.

She wished it wasn't true, that she didn't have to go on hurting like this for ever, never able to stop without the loneliness welling up and drowning her.

As the water streamed down over her shoulders, she was abruptly enveloped by a brief fantasy that Scott was in the next room waiting for her.

How many times did she have to lose him?

Once in reality. For ever in her mind.

Did Lyle feel like this about Hazel? She hoped not, she didn't want those eyes to conceal such a painful, desperate loneliness.

She scrubbed her hair hard under the pounding water, washing the last traces of the sea away, soaping every part of her body that could bear to be touched. She had red marks and black and purple marks that would be with her for a long time, but she was alive and it was time to get active, get away from the misery and self-pity that seemed to go with being stuck in bed.

Lyle was nowhere in sight when she came out of the bathroom, but he had left a soft jogging-suit that must be Dorothy's on her bed. She pulled it on thankfully. She thought she could get away without a new bandage on her leg if she stuck to soft, loose trousers for a while.

The house was empty. She moved down a long corridor, past the room that must be Lyle's.

A warm room, in brown and rust and gold. Masculine, yet comfortable. A big mirror on an oak wardrobe reflected a lighthouse painting, with waves crashing on the rocks. On another wall, a modern rendition of colours communicated a strong mood, although she couldn't have identified the subject matter of the painting. The modern and the traditional, mixed together.

The more she learned about Lyle, the more she liked. If it weren't for this restless need to move on, she might have been able to enjoy getting to know him better.

But it was too easy to think here, too easy to let her emotions get the better of her. She kept having dreams that brought Scott back. She'd managed to keep control ever since Scott had died. She certainly couldn't let go now.

A book lay open on Lyle's bedside table. George resisted the temptation to step closer and read its title.

Robin's room next, its door open on a profusion of stuffed animals. A big orange cat stretched and rested its head on the back of a stuffed bear as George passed.

The living-room was filled with books, cassette tapes and records. She browsed through them, finding all her favourites. There was classical music, too, but she had never developed much of an ear for classical. She loved guitar music of almost any sort, loved playing the guitar herself, and she was going to ask Lyle if he minded her playing some of these tapes while she was here.

Most of the tapes were commercial ones, but some were labelled by hand, in a firm handwriting that she knew would belong to Lyle. It was like him. Square and even, with a flourish here and there. The song titles written in his hand intrigued her. They must be special favourites of his.

The books were a surprising assortment. Some of the books were on music, more on flying. An assortment of novels that ranged from Robert Ludlum to Ernest Hemingway. Children's books, some on how to raise rabbits.

Rabbits? Here on Green Island?

A book of poems by Tennyson.

Two copies of a volume entitled *Verses in Flight*, by Lyle Stevens.

Lyle?

She took one off the shelf, opened it and found the dedication. *For my daughter Robin.*

She sank down on a big overstuffed chair, turning the pages slowly. Poems of flying, verses of love for his family and the animals he took under his wing.

Dreamer's eyes, she'd thought. Poet's eyes.

When she looked up and saw him standing there, it wasn't a surprise.

'I found your book,' she said slowly, her eyes far off.

He sat on the arm of the chair, leaning over to read with her, bracing his arm on the chair behind her head. She could smell the tangy scent of aftershave and wondered why a man out in the middle of nowhere would bother to use a tangy aftershave lotion. For her?

'I wrote that one in Stewart,' he said, reading over her shoulder. 'Glacier country. They were shooting a movie and I was flying people around, taking them up to the glacier, and back down.'

'Tell me about it,' she invited eagerly.

He grinned. 'It *was* fun. What an insane bunch of running around they do for this movie business! And money flowing like water. The studio spent a fortune on helicopter time—spent a fortune on everything.'

He named the movie.

'I remember seeing that! There were helicopters *in* the movie too, weren't there? Were you flying in any of them?'

'Yes. In one scene—the rescue scene.'

'You mean the avalanche?' The book went slack in her hands as she twisted to see his face. 'That must have been dangerous flying!'

He nodded, his eyes sparkling with the memory. 'It was risky, all right.' He laughed. 'My brief run as a stunt man! My mother gave me hell when she saw the movie, but I wasn't married at the time, didn't have Robin. There was no one depending on me.'

'So it was all right to risk your life?' Her voice sharpened and he chuckled. He took the book from her hands and tipped her chin up so he could see into her eyes.

'You sounded a bit like my mother there,' he teased her. 'You're hardly the lady to talk sharp about people risking their lives, are you? Single-handing a sail-boat through some of the most dangerous waters in the world!'

'But I had no intention of killing myself at it.' Nor had he, of course. 'You come from a big family, don't you? A close family.'

'Not that big. My parents, and three of us. Russ and I, and Conrad. Con's my older brother.'

She shifted, drawing her legs up and turning so that she could see his face without strain. He was relaxed, leaning back on the arm that rested so close to her head. 'And you're all close?' she asked.

'So so,' he told her, grinning. 'Russ and I get on OK, but Con and I always fought. He was bigger than me, but I usually didn't have the sense to stay out of his way. I used to tease him, drive him nuts. Then he'd lose his cool and clobber me. Nowadays I stay out of his way. We see each other at Christmas. Last time I saw him was at Russ's wedding. We got into an argument and Mom threw us out of the house to cool off.'

'Is he married?'

'Oh, yes. And I may not be scared of Con any more, but I'm sure as hell terrified of Betty! She's almost six foot, never a hair out of place, and a voice like a sergeant major. They've got two kids—a boy and a girl—who never have a hair out of place, either. I keep having the urge to take them out fishing, get them covered with seaweed and smelling of fish, then bring them home. Con would never forgive me, but I'm sure the kids would be better for a bit of dirt and adventure.'

His hand had dropped to her shoulder and was kneading gently. She found herself relaxing against his arm. 'It sounds nice,' she said slowly. 'Robin told me about your parents. They live on a farm near Victoria, don't they?'

'Not exactly a farm. A couple of acres, kind of a hobby farm. They're retired and puttering around. When we were kids we lived on a lighthouse further up Vancouver Island, but my parents bought the Victoria property when I was in my teens. After that, we always went there for holidays. That's a habit we've all kept over the years. Robin and I still go down there for at least a few days every year.'

She was smiling until he said, 'You'd like them—you'd like my family, I mean. And they'd like you. Especially my father.'

Lyle wanted to tell her that he would take her to see them, but the urge frightened him a little, and he knew it wasn't time yet. 'Tell me about your family, George.' She shrugged and winced and he said, quickly, 'Are you all right? Those ribs still hurt?'

She shook her head, shifting away from his touch. She'd been enjoying talking to him—until he'd started asking questions.

She didn't want to talk about her family. They were nice people but, except for Jenny, there was no one who gave her a feeling of homecoming. And talking about her family would lead to Scott.

When she moved, the dog moved too, his toes clicking on the kitchen floor as he padded towards them. He stopped in front of them, placing his head carefully on George's lap. She stroked him. Her hand came away covered with dog hair.

'He needs a good brushing,' said Lyle, shifting to his feet. 'I'll get the brush.'

George relaxed, relieved that the subject was changed. She wasn't going to have to fence with Lyle, trying to

avoid talking about Jenny and Mom and—inevitably—
Scott.

When Lyle handed her the brush, she started brushing
the dog firmly. Scruff sagged against her leg with a groan
that was either pleasure or pain.

Lyle said gently, 'George, you'll have to talk about it
all some day. You can't shut everything in.'

She found herself breathing shallowly, her eyes chal-
lenging his as if there were a threat, as if she mustn't let
him closer.

It was a long moment before he shifted, breaking
contact with her eyes. 'I have a weather broadcast to do.
Robin's next door at Russ's place. You look after Scruff,
and we'll both be back in a bit.'

Thank goodness he'd gone!

Some crazy part of her wanted to share everything
with him, to go into his arms and feel them close around
her, strong and secure. She wanted to tell him all her
problems, her hurts, and let him make everything right.

Was she insane? Going through a second childhood?

Or was it Lyle himself? Was it the strength of the man's
personality, making her feel the warmth of his presence,
even when he left the room?

He was a man who should have a wife and a big family.
She could see him calmly managing an unruly pile of
children and animals, writing poems in the quiet moments and, somewhere in it all, flying that airplane into
the skies.

She had never had an animal, had never realised how
much hair could come out of the coat of a dog that was
part Husky and part many other things. Scruff groaned
and stretched, pushing against the brush. George stopped
when her arms were aching.

Who had told her about someone spinning the hair
of a Husky dog and making a sweater of it? She giggled,
trying to picture Lyle doing that.

She found the bin in the kitchen and threw away Scruff's hair.

The house was quiet, except for the faint noise of wind from outside. She could see the ocean through the windows. What a city dweller wouldn't give for a view like this! But what city dweller would be willing to pay the price in remote isolation?

In the kitchen, an oil stove beckoned to her with promises of warmth. Outside was the wild.

She'd been too long indoors.

She found a warm Mackinaw hanging near the stove. The sleeves were too long, but she rolled them up and prowled through the porch, looking for shoes. A windy March day was no time to be without shoes.

In the end she gave up the search, going barefoot, hopping to keep her feet out of the way of Scruff's paws when the dog suddenly realised he was being left behind and scrabbled to catch up to her as she went through the door.

She couldn't imagine this dog bearing the respectable name of Harry. Robin had been right to name him Scruff.

She walked downstairs into the midst of a noisy cluster of buildings. What was the racket? Electricity being generated?

The lighthouse tower stood tall and white between the two houses, a prominent landmark to warn mariners of the rocks around Green Island.

Rocks. *Lady Harriet*, about to hit the rocks...

No! Think about something else. The buildings. Light tower, engine-room—that must be the second house, where Lyle's brother lived. Robin was there right now, inside that house. Lyle was giving a weather report, but where?

Spooky. Empty. As if there were no one else in the world. Through every crack between the buildings, all around her, was the ocean. She could feel it, smell it.

She was on the edge of the world. Alone.

She would be alone all her life.

Lyle had his family, his animals. Russ had his wife and the baby they were expecting.

George didn't belong here. She had no one. She should leave, get back to the world, get moving again.

She prowled around the buildings, forcing the restlessness, getting her mind ready for leaving and doing whatever it was she was going to do next.

She walked around the outside of the engine-room, on to some kind of wooden platform that was built out over the edge of a cliff. She tuned out the roar of the engines, concentrated on the wind howling over the rocks.

She couldn't hear him, but she knew when Lyle came up behind her.

'I had to get outside.' She twisted to look up into his face, looking for anger but finding none.

'What about the leg?' He was watching her, his eyes narrowed as if they could tell more than he would learn from her answer. She shifted her bare feet self-consciously.

'My leg's OK. The weather's better, isn't it?' She turned away from him, waving an arm towards the water, wishing she didn't feel like an awkward teenager, wishing she weren't so aware of him.

His eyes stayed on her face. He could feel her unease, but wasn't sure what was causing it. He said, 'It's still pretty rough. I don't think you'd want to be sailing.'

She shuddered. She turned away as if to reject the memory, but couldn't keep from asking, 'Is that where she went down? That rock to the north?'

'Yes,' he answered, remembering how her face had looked just after he'd pulled her out of the water.

'I'm lucky to be alive, aren't I?' She looked up at him. He didn't know what she was looking for. He had an uncomfortable feeling that she was comparing him to her husband. He disliked the idea intensely.

She finally looked away, frowning. Lyle wished he could catch her hand and draw her closer. He'd like to stand here with his arm around her, looking out over the wild Pacific, feeling her against his side.

He moved a little closer, sheltering her from the wind, but he could feel her tension at his nearness.

George glanced up at him. He was waiting for her to step away. She stood carefully still. It seemed important that he believe she was not bothered by his nearness.

He was standing so close. She felt his height, the strong breadth of his shoulders.

Scott hadn't been as tall. His masculinity had been more civilised, more—more predictable. George's eyes swung back to Lyle, tracing the hard curves of his face, the surprising softness of his lips. She almost imagined she could remember Lyle's arms pulling her from the cold sea. It was that uncertain memory that made her uncomfortable enough to step away.

'I can't believe you spotted me out there in the water.'

'Luck,' he said harshly. The lines on his face suddenly stood out painfully.

Then he smiled, his eyes lighting with a challenge that struck a chord of memory.

'Lyle, you—you weren't by any chance at the Holiday Inn last year? In Vancouver? I was booked in a room on the second floor, and you—you had a room on the same floor. We passed in the hall once. Then, when I had dinner with Jenny, my cousin, and you were sitting——'

He'd been wearing a brown suit, and Jenny had said something like, 'You've made a conquest there,' while George had tried to pretend those disturbing eyes weren't watching her.

'You probably don't remember,' George said hurriedly, wishing she hadn't started this. 'Maybe it wasn't——'

'I remember.' His eyes were giving her a disturbing message, as they had that day in the corridor. 'I recognised you as soon as I pulled you out of the ocean.'

'In a cruiser suit!' She turned away to cover the flush that she felt surging into her face and neck.

He wanted her. He'd wanted her from the beginning. Was that why she'd been so aware of him?

Incredibly, part of her wanted to respond, to meet his eyes and answer the invitation with her own wordless acceptance.

She mustn't! She was too weak, too vulnerable. In Mexico, the problem had been that she felt nothing. With Lyle, here on this island, she was in danger of feeling too much. If he took her in his arms, she was so mixed up and confused that she might close her eyes and lose herself in the dream.

She couldn't use his arms to pretend she had Scott back. She must never do that!

She pushed her hands into her pockets, managing to laugh and throw him a bright, superficial glance. 'I'm not sure I'm flattered at your recognising me. I must have been better dressed at the Holiday Inn!'

He saw right through the brittle brightness, and said, 'You looked a bit like you do now. Like a wild thing, afraid of captivity.'

Startled, she jerked back. His hand shot out and grasped her arm, pulling her away from the edge of the platform.

'Watch——'

'It's OK,' she said breathlessly, pulling away from his touch. 'I—I really think it's time I left. I appreciate all you've done, but I should——'

He was watching her, seeing too much.

'Where are you going?' he demanded insistently. 'What's the hurry?'

She looked around desperately. Somewhere, anywhere. Surely it didn't matter, so long as she got away from here.

'Couldn't you get a float-plane in here for me? You could radio. I'd pay, of course.'

'With what?' He leaned against the hoist as if he were settling in for a long inquisition. 'You didn't arrive here with your wallet in your pocket.'

She had nothing. Her jeans and shirt. A torn cruiser suit. She pushed down the panic, said, 'I—any bank. I just have to get to a bank.'

'No identification?' He looked away from her, his narrowed eyes searching the water. 'Banks are a bit awkward about giving money if you can't prove who you are.'

She glanced around helplessly, then back at Lyle. He was doing this deliberately, making it hard for her. Her chest tightened in an unwelcome urge to cry. She sucked in a deep breath, forced anger. 'I was shipwrecked! If you explained that, surely you could find a seaplane company that would be willing to fly me in to Prince Rupert and wait a couple of hours for their money! I could go to the bank, or I could call Jenny and get her to arrange some money for me!'

He shook his head. 'You couldn't get a seaplane out here. Not in that kind of sea.'

'But——' George swung around to the wild ocean. Surely there was some way to get out of here! She was ready to go. She had to go—quickly!

'What if there were an emergency? Surely a helicopter, or a boat——'

'There was an emergency.' He was looking down at her. He seemed suddenly even taller. 'The other night, when I fished you in out of the sea I'd have given anything to be able to get you to a hospital. It was impossible. There was no way anyone could get near this island—not safely.'

He touched her arm. She jerked away. She had a wild need to strike out, to hit him and run to some safe retreat where she could pull a net of seclusion around herself. She hugged herself tightly, glaring at him.

His voice had the same tone he might use on a frightened animal. 'Take it easy, George. There's not really any urgency, is there?'

'I have to go!'

'Why? Where?'

She glanced around wildly. The sea and the buildings. She was terrified, panic-stricken, without knowing why or what. 'Vancouver,' she said abruptly. 'Jenny. I'll go to Jenny.'

'Who's Jenny?' His voice was low and quiet. She began to lose some of her panic, to breathe more easily.

'Jenny's my cousin.' She closed her eyes, feeling some of the fear draining away. 'I think I'm a bit crazy,' she said unsteadily, realising how she must sound. 'I don't know what got into me.'

His eyes were tender. 'You've had a shock, you've been shipwrecked, suffered hypothermia and a thorough bashing on the rocks. Your mind and your body are still trying to come to terms with it all.'

She didn't resist when he drew her against his side, but found herself leaning against him, drawing his strength.

'I'll go to Jenny.'

'Would she look after you?' He turned her away from the water, started her moving towards his house. 'You're not ready to be wandering around alone. There isn't really any place that's home, is there?'

Jenny wasn't home. George loved Jenny, but she'd paid a flying visit before she came north and her cousin had been far too busy to take on a convalescent guest.

Lyle saw her smile and she had to explain, 'The last time I saw Jenny, she—she and Jake have this media business, and Jenny was in the studio putting together a new documentary on the Queen Charlottes. She had a pen in one hand, and the baby—they just had a baby—in her arm, nursing. And Jake was bombing in with equipment hanging all over him. They were getting ready to fly north on location—baby and all! No, of course I won't go to Jenny.' But she really must go somewhere. 'I'll go to my mother, in Campbell River.'

'Will you?' Before she knew what he was doing, before she could protest, he had leaned down and slipped his arms under her legs and back, picking her up in his arms as if she were no weight at all.

'Put me down!' She tried to sound outraged, but her body betrayed her and sagged against his chest, welcoming the support of his arms.

He held her close against his chest. 'I've watched you shivering long enough. We'll go inside. Next time you go out, for God's sake put something on your feet!'

'Please put me down!'

'I rescued you from the sea! I'm damned if I'll let you die of pneumonia! Not while I'm looking after you!'

'I'm not one of your strays!' George glared at his chin. She tried to ignore her thundering heart, hoped he couldn't hear it. 'I want to get off this island! You can't keep me here by force!'

'That's an idea,' said Lyle speculatively, laughing down at her. 'You're warm and soft and—are you sure you're not a stray?' She felt his muscles tense, holding her more securely as he started up the stairs with her in his arms. 'Open that door, will you? I've got my hands full!'

She glared at that unyielding chin, met eyes that held both laughter and desire.

He—no, it was insane! He wouldn't keep her here, as if she were a cat without a home!

'Why should I open the door?' she demanded aggressively. She was at a definite disadvantage, held in his strong arms, but she'd never hesitated to get into a fight. 'I asked you to put me down. You can wait all day if you want me to open the door when I don't even want to be carried!'

'All right,' he agreed with deceptive co-operation. He shifted, leaning his hips against the porch rail, drawing one leg up slightly to support some of her weight.

She was even closer to him now, cradled against his chest, his lips only inches away from hers. She tried to look away, but there wasn't anywhere to look.

'Will you let me go? I'm not a——'

'A stray?' he finished softly. 'But you don't have a home, do you? Shall I take you in?' She froze as his lips brushed against her forehead. 'Yes, I think I should,' he whispered against her soft skin.

'Please let me down, Lyle.' She pushed against his chest, feeling the hard muscles through his jacket. She was afraid that he might win, that she might lose the ability to resist, and melt into his arms instead. What would it feel like to touch his bare chest with her hands?

'As soon as you open the door,' he agreed pleasantly. 'I'm not putting you down out here in bare feet.'

'And I'm not opening the door!'

He laughed, revealing very straight, white teeth. 'Well, I'll certainly enjoy holding you in my arms meanwhile. George, you're not a very compliant guest. Did you argue with your husband all the time?'

'We didn't argue at all,' she said witheringly. 'Will you shut up and——'

'Not at all?' he asked disbelievingly. 'Just what kind of a relationship—whoops! Watch out!' He moved swiftly as the door opened towards them, taking her whole weight in his arms again, ducking around the edge of the door.

George looked away from his laughing blue eyes, down into a his daughter's paler blue eyes.

'Thanks, Robin,' said Lyle as he walked into the house with George still trapped in his arms. 'I was wondering how I'd get that door open.'

'Where are my shoes?' she demanded as he set her down on the carpet in the living-room.

'In the pantry. Behind the kitchen. I'll get them.'

When he was gone, George sank weakly on to the big easy chair. Robin followed her, standing beside the chair. 'Did your leg get tired? Did Daddy have to carry you home?'

'I——' She met Robin's curious eyes and didn't know what to say except, 'Your daddy thought my feet were cold. I went out without shoes.'

'Sometimes Daddy carries me home.'

Robin was surely her father's daughter, determined to look after the strays of the world, and somehow certain that George qualified as one of those that needed looking after.

She let Robin settle her on the chesterfield, warm her with a blanket, and found herself admitting that she was exhausted.

'Have a nap,' her young nurse ordered. 'You've gotta rest your leg.'

She didn't open her eyes again until she heard the cat growling.

Robin was sitting cross-legged on the floor, pulling on a string that snaked across the carpet.

Dixie lay near the end of the string, tail twitching, eyes following the movement, a low growl coming from her throat.

Robin gave a sharp jerk to the string. Dixie pounced, claws bared. The string slipped through her paw. She hissed at it, then flattened herself on the carpet, motionless except for the tail.

Lyle was seated at a desk, his brow heavily furrowed as he stared down at a pad of paper in front of him.

'Hi,' said Robin softly.

'Hello yourself,' said George.

Lyle looked up from the troublesome pad in front of him. 'Feeling better?' he asked, smiling as his eyes met hers.

'Yes,' she admitted, her own lips curving. 'That cat has an odd stomach.'

Robin giggled. Lyle said, 'She's pregnant. When we got the cats, we thought they were both male, but Dixie has recently proven us wrong. Could you eat supper? Robin and I were thinking about food.'

'I could eat a horse,' she decided, sitting up and rubbing the sleep from her eyes. 'Could I help with something?'

Robin made the supper—prepared dinners heated in the microwave—while George set the table. They ate at the kitchen table, the window beside George open to the rocky shore and the ocean. Outside the window was a plastic receptacle filled with coloured liquid.

'Humming-bird feeder,' said Robin.

'Do humming-birds really come to it?' George bent her head out the window to look closer. 'What's the liquid?'

'Water,' said Lyle, 'coloured with food colouring and flavoured with sugar. The birds hover at the feeder, almost like a helicopter. But you won't see them today. You'll have to wait till later in the spring.'

She would be gone before the birds came.

Robin explained lighthouses to her while Lyle listened, amused, putting in a comment here and there.

Groceries only once a month, delivered usually by helicopter, sometimes by ship. No telephone. No roads.

'But we got television,' said Robin. 'If you want to watch TV you can. And radio. And lots of books. And soon the fishermen will come and collect gull eggs.'

Lyle explained, 'Some of the natives like to eat seagull eggs. A colony of seagulls nest in the rocks at the other end of the island. And you needn't worry about the baby gulls. The females do lay again when the eggs disappear from the nest.'

'Daddy?' Robin interrupted. 'It's weather time.'

'Right.' He stood with a smooth motion. 'I'll be back in a few minutes. I've got a weather broadcast to give.'

Would he really keep her here, preventing her departure by simply refusing to help her go?

Later they played Trivial Pursuit—the Junior Edition. George was amazed when she won the game. 'Mainly because you kept giving me hints,' she accused Robin.

The girl said simply, 'I wanted you to win.'

'Well, don't do it next time. You shouldn't let other people win if they don't deserve it. Make me fight for it next time.'

Lyle was watching them with a quiet smile.

As if she were his woman.

She wasn't anybody's woman. Never again.

CHAPTER FOUR

GEORGE twisted restlessly in her sleep. The mournful wail of the foghorn blended with the sound of wind and water, reinforcing the strength of her dream...

The small ship shuddered as it came down from a steep wave. She held tightly on to the wheel, wincing as green water crashed along the deck, sending a hard sheet of spray over the cockpit.

She had been clinging desperately to the steering wheel for hours. She badly wanted something to eat, even a drink of water. She didn't dare let go the wheel in these seas.

She was travelling north. Alone. Going with the wind.

Fresh waves had turned to wild, angry monsters, tossing her boat mercilessly, leaving her helplessly clinging to a wheel that couldn't be handled by her small, sturdy muscles.

The wind tore at the waves, throwing water across the cockpit, smashing her in the face. Changing sails on deck in the midst of a gale.

Then, disaster. *Lady Harriet* went wild, heeling over sharply.

The auto-pilot was steering her in circles! George stumbled into the navigation room to fight with the override button, trying to get *Lady Harriet* back off the wind.

'You can't sail it alone!' her mother had wailed the year before.

'Why not?' she'd demanded heatedly. 'With an auto-pilot, and winches on all the sails I shall be fine. An auto-pilot is like having another crew member, you know.'

'Damn you, Otto!' George muttered at the inanimate black box of electronics. 'I never counted on your getting sick!'

What would Scott have done? He'd been the captain, the one who made all the decisions. She was insane, crazy to think she could sail these waters alone!

Too much sail up for this wind. If only she had someone to handle the wheel while she got sails down.

Lady Harriet leaned over wildly, throwing her off balance.

Fighting the wheel, leaning hard against the spokes, taking the sharp edge against her side in an attempt to make her slight frame do the work of a man's as the ship's spreaders almost dipped into the water, George hung on desperately, fighting a terrifying urge to let go of the wheel and give up.

Hold...hold...pull the wheel a fraction of an inch as the wind eased for a second. Then, suddenly, *Lady Harriet* was righted, running downwind in a swaying, surfing ride that was deceptively easy.

As each big wave swept up her stern, the vessel tried to twist, broaching on the waves. George was steering left, then right, trying to correct each wild swing before it occurred.

Get me out of this!

No one heard.

Oh, God! Why? What was she doing here? Where was Scott? Would the wind ever stop?

Where was she? Near Green Island? Shouldn't she see the light? Green Island...what had it been like on the chart? A tiny island. Rocks. There was shelter farther north, around the top of Dundas Island. There was a bay—damn! She couldn't remember. The chart was inside.

Could she lash the wheel in position?

Her arms were aching, legs burning from too many hours braced against the sides of the cockpit.

A moment of dizziness.

Then Scott, standing beside her, tall and strong. Thank God!

Her hands slackened on the wheel, her lips curving in a smile. She stepped back to let him take over. He was gone, dissolved into waves and pelting rain. Cold. Wet.

Another harebrained adventure, her mother would say.

This could be the last one. If she drowned, would she be with Scott again?

If only she could let go, give up.

She hung on, squeezing her eyes shut as the water crashed over her again.

Where in God's name was she?

What was that dark shadow? There! It—— No, gone again!

Was she clear of the rocks? She couldn't see. She'd tried to steer a compass course, but the waves were getting bigger, monsters surging under the stern, lifting her high, shooting *Lady Harriet* forward in an uncontrolled roller-coaster ride.

If that——

Lady Harriet went wild, sweeping up on a mountainous monster wave, shooting across the surface like a paper ship.

The wheel spun in her hands like a toy.

Water loud and white, all around.

Rocks!

The radio! If she called for help——What ——

Raging water, white and black. She lost her grip on the wheel, went flying, arms and legs spread, desperately grasping for a hold on something, anything.

She was going to die!

Lyle stumbled out of bed, half-asleep.

He groped for a bathrobe, belted it over his naked form as he crossed the hallway.

She had twisted her blankets into a tangle. The sweep of the light showed her face, briefly, tight with fear, her eyes closed, lips moving.

...giant waves...wind...steering.

He'd tried to get her to talk about the shipwreck, but she'd been pushing it down, trying not to remember. Now her mind had taken over, was forcing her to relive the worst moments.

He sat down beside her, gathered her close. She fought him, trying to twist free. Then, abruptly, she came, soft and trembling, into his arms. He looked down at her closed eyes, felt the beginnings of another bad spot in her dream and held her close. He wasn't sure he wanted to feel like this. He'd only known her a few days, but he loved her.

She was restless and wild. Exciting. If he tried to win her, his life was going to change and he'd have little control over the changes.

He felt her distress, felt the same terrible helplessness that came over him when Robin was hurt and he couldn't take away her pain.

'George...'

She wouldn't hear him, but he kept his arms close around her, holding her, stroking her back, trying to bring her back from the memories.

Cold invading her bones. Then warmth.

Arms holding her, sheltering her.

Scott.

He was touching her, rousing her with gentle stroking.

His arms dropped away. She reached out, pleading.

He frowned, stepping back, leaving her cold and alone.

She cried out as he faded.

The foghorn wailed across the island, sending a warning to mariners.

Her hand on the cold, white telephone receiver.

Scott...heart attack...hospital. No! Please, no!

Her thundering heart was drowning out the voice. Who? No! She couldn't lose him! She mustn't—couldn't bear it if he left her!

He'd brought love. He was her life. She needed him, couldn't lose him. Oh, God! Please don't take Scott away!

Her mother, frowning, her voice punishing with its useless pity. *I warned you, Georgina! He was too old for you. I warned you.*

Hospital.

No! Don't leave me! I'll do whatever you want, be whoever you want. Please don't go away and leave me alone again!

Cold. Empty. She twisted, fought arms that held her, felt the wetness of her tears as her face moved against cool skin.

A low, husky voice, 'Easy, darling. Easy. You're OK.'

Cold night air on her skin. A man's warm body against hers.

Lyle's face. Lyle's hands, soothing her heated skin. She was in Lyle's house, Lyle's guest bedroom. Scott was gone. For ever.

'Hey,' he whispered softly, his hand brushing the wetness away from her cheek. 'Don't cry, honey. You had a dream. A nightmare.' He gathered her closer into his arms and she found herself cradled against his warm, broad chest.

'Were you dreaming about the shipwreck?'

She shuddered. Scott. Scott was gone for ever.

The doctor, standing uncomfortably in the waiting-room, saying, 'I'm sorry, Mrs Dobson.'

He'd never take her in his arms again.

His hands stroking her back, the warmth and the closeness . . .

Lyle's hands on her back, lips softly kissing her cheek where the tears had started to dry. Outside, the foghorn wailed. George shuddered, burrowing herself deeper into his arms. Her sobs slowly quietened. Her hand crept up, flattening itself against his bare, warm chest.

He moved, murmuring, 'Here, honey, just shift a little.'

She shook her head drowsily, drifting away from the voice, burrowing against the warmth, seeking comfort and closeness instinctively. Scott...

'That's better,' he murmured, gathering her against him, pulling the covers back over them both as she shivered again. 'Isn't it?' he continued, watching her, keeping his voice low, not wanting to alarm her, but wanting to draw her out of the nightmare.

'Don't talk,' she whispered, turning towards him, letting her palm brush against the hairs on his chest. Her body curved against his length, her soft thigh brushed his muscular one.

A deep shudder went through her.

'Honey, are you sure you know what you're doing?'

The wrong voice. Too deep. Too young.

Warm.

The hurting would come back if she lost the warmth. She whispered, 'Please don't talk,' without knowing what she said.

Her hand moved rhythmically against his skin, drawing comfort from his heat.

She curled closer, a soft, clinging warmth against his hard maleness. He was still, his arms against her back until she turned, bringing his hand over her breast.

His hand trembled, then closed on the softness.

She let go her tenuous grip on reality, welcoming the tide of feeling that grew as his hand cupped the fullness.

She sent her messages to him softly, silently, as Scott had taught her, moving against him without words, waiting, wanting, until he moved his hands along the soft woman curves of her. Then she was trembling for him, aching with need.

His hand smoothed over the thrust of her hip, his mouth bent to her breast, drawing the taut hardness of her nipple softly between his lips.

She whispered his name as she went spinning through the tide of passion rising around her.

His hands tensed, suddenly rough and hard on her body. Then she was alone, cold, shivering.

Her eyes opened, glazed with her fantasy, staring up.

'Wake up, George!' His voice was harsh, cold.

Their eyes locked. She saw intimate knowledge of her body in his eyes, felt the flush on her skin from his touch.

'My name is Lyle.' His voice whipped over her. He stared down at her body lying exposed and pale in the light that swept across the window. 'And I don't need a woman so badly that I'm about to act the part of a dead man.'

He turned and strode away, slamming her bedroom door closed as he went, leaving her alone.

Scott.

She closed her eyes, still shivering with the cold air, even after she pulled the covers over her heated body. She lay alone, staring at the picture on the wall as the lighthouse light swept over it, then left it dark.

She felt the hot tide of shame rising as she lived again the feel of Lyle's hands on her skin, remembered how she had shut out the sound of his voice as it intruded on her fantasy.

Scott had been making love to her. It was Scott's name she had cried out as Lyle's lips took possession of her breast.

For the first time since Scott's death, her tears flowed freely, racking her body until she was spent, empty, lying alone on the bed in the darkness.

An endless time awake, her mind almost blank. Then, slowly, she started to hear the night noises of the house. The creaking of a step. Lyle. The fading echo as a door slammed. He was gone now. Outside. She stared at her door in the dark, feeling closed in, shut out.

Each night Lyle had left the door to her room open so that he could hear her if she called out in the night.

Tonight she had called out, and he had come.

How could she have lain in his arms, silently asking him to make love to her?

What must he think of her? In her mind the dream was mixed with the reality, but she remembered enough to know that she had invited his caresses, his lips on her skin. The memory of his touch had a heat that her dreams of Scott had never had.

What was he doing now? Was he walking to cool off? There was no doubt he had been aroused. She'd seen his body all too clearly as he stood beside the bed, knew it was her own hands that had undone the belt of his robe. How could she?

She had to get off this island. There was no way she could face him after this, looking into his eyes, remembering how she had tried to pretend he was Scott, begging him to make her his.

The door again. Footsteps. He was back, in the basement. Would he go to bed now?

Silence. Then the faint sounds of music, muted. Pieces of a song, strung together, repeated, haunting notes floating on the night air. Where was the music coming from? She listened, lying alone.

Ever since her father had died, she had been the outsider, the one who didn't belong. She'd laughed, and moved on, but there had never been a place that was really hers. Even with Scott——

She had tried so hard, but she'd never quite been what he wanted her to be. In the end he had left her with a finality that she had no weapons against.

Left her? How could she think of Scott's death as a wilful abandonment? As if both Scott and her father had rejected her through some choice. She needed a psychiatrist. No! She wasn't going to turn her insecurities inside out for some clinical expert to frown at.

Lyle was somewhere. With the music.

Only moments ago she'd tried to make him into a fantasy to heal her pain. Now she was moving again, getting up, hoping to push away the memories with his presence.

She couldn't stay alone here another minute. If she were in a city she would get her guitar and go out, take a taxi to a coffee house and try to drown memories in music.

She was alone and miserable. She couldn't resist the sound of music.

If she was going to get up, she had to wear something more conventional than an oversized sweatshirt and bare legs. She slipped out of bed, her bare feet silent on the braided carpet. The dresser drawer slipped open easily. She wasn't really surprised to find her own jeans lying inside, freshly washed and neatly folded.

A complete change of clothes. Jeans and shirt, underwear and bra. She slipped into them. She even put on the bra, although it hurt where it hugged her left side. The denim jeans hurt, too, against the partly healed gash on her leg.

She padded silently to the bathroom, combing her hair and washing her face, trying to get rid of the sleepy-eyed look that might remind him of what had happened in her bedroom only moments ago.

If she had any sense, she'd be staying in bed, going to sleep and pretending tonight had never happened. Facing Lyle was going to be embarrassing.

Her bare feet were silent on the carpeted hallway. She was sure he wouldn't hear her from the basement.

Robin's door was open. A night-light on the wall threw soft illumination over the sleeping girl, her long hair spread out over her pillow in a tangle that must be a nightmare to comb out in the morning.

The sight of the sleeping girl reminded George too intensely of her own childlessness. She turned away.

The music was hauntingly faint.

The living-room was dark and silent, lighted only by the lighthouse beam as it shone in the windows.

In the shadowy kitchen, the big orange cat stood up and stretched, staring as George passed.

The fourth stair creaked loudly as she went down to the basement. At the bottom, the concrete floor was shockingly cold underfoot.

A freezer. Washing machine. She slipped through an open door and found herself in the radio-room. It was dark and empty.

Only one door left. Closed.

There was a piece of paper taped to it, a childishly drawn sign that said, *Daddy's room*.

She took a deep breath before she opened the door.

He heard the creak of the step. It always creaked, and he'd always intended to fix it.

He wanted to go out to her, take her in his arms and bring her here, warm her and love her——

Last year she'd been only a passing dream, stirring yearnings. He'd seen her with that flash of recognition that comes only rarely, the intuitive knowledge that another person could be someone special.

Could be... Did saving her life give him some mystical claim to her? Or was it the other way? That she had a claim on him? She was even getting tangled into his music.

Tangled in his life. Damn! He didn't need this! There were other women—women with free hearts.

His hand jerked on the synthesiser.

Just another woman who didn't really want him.

The music shuddered in a discordant wobble.

She belonged to a dead man. His name was Scott.

Had Scott loved her going barefoot on the cold rocks? Had he——

Stop it! Jealous of a dead man?

The door opened. He saw her come in and knew that the wrong word would send her away—and he didn't want to send her away.

She closed the door behind herself. He dropped his eyes to the synthesiser, brought the volume up a little as she took in his room.

Thick carpet everywhere, even on the walls. Would she think that strange? He'd had to deaden the sound to allow recording without too much contamination from outside noises. Even the windows were covered. He'd used fibreglass insulation bats, then covered it all with blankets.

The song was coming. He had the drums recorded. He was working on the bass guitar now, making the music with his fingers on the synthesiser, rather than using his guitar. He was far better with the synthesiser than with a real instrument.

His feet were controlling the volume with the variable pedal on the floor. He had the sound coming through the four big monitor speakers on the wall, although the bass guitar track was recording directly from the synthesiser to the multi-track recorder.

She was leaning against the closed door. She looked tired, vulnerable. She was wearing her jeans. He hoped the denim wasn't too harsh on the newly healed cut on her leg. He saw the thrust of her breasts that revealed she was wearing a bra over her bruised ribs, and he knew why. It was a message for him, whether she realised it or not. A barrier.

She had the nervous look of a frightened animal, ready to bolt.

And he still wanted her.

He wasn't giving up so easily, although he had more than a dead husband to contend with. George wasn't roaming the seas just from grief. She was a wild thing, needing love, yet afraid of the warmth.

He knew how to deal with wild things. It took time, and love. He wouldn't make the mistake he'd made with Hazel, wouldn't trap her with demands and declarations. She'd be free, and one day she would choose to stay.

She was restless already, and he wouldn't be able to keep her here. He'd have to find a way to keep contact, to give her time.

He felt a sudden wave of hopelessness. Too little time. She'd slip away. He'd lose her. For ever.

Her eyes met his. Hers were uncertain. He tried to keep the heat out of his. He looked away, concentrated on the beat of the music, on completing the rhythm.

He felt her coming closer, but he didn't look up. He could see her without looking directly at her. She was curled up on the end of the sofa, sitting tense as she listened and watched.

When she closed her eyes and leaned her head back, he knew that the music was what she wanted. He drifted away then, caught up in developing the song, although he could still feel her there every second.

He jotted a note on the page in front of him, working on that difficult passage, the transition that didn't seem to work. He stumbled over it, rewound the tape and approached it again, trying to get the right feel for it.

After the first few minutes, George realised that Lyle wasn't going to flash anger and rejection at her with those deep blue eyes. She didn't know why she'd come down to him, but she knew she had no right to seek companionship from him after the rejection she'd just given. But she was here, regardless.

She let the music take possession of her.

It was a catchy tune. The rhythm had that irresistible something that hit songs seemed to have. She thought there should be words, too. She thought of his poems and she hummed softly, fitting wordless sounds to music. Her fingers itched to pick out the rhythm on a guitar.

She saw the guitar sitting idle in the corner. He seemed deeply intent on the sounds he was making, his eyes far away as his ears listened critically. She certainly couldn't interrupt him.

She smiled a little, watching his absorption. Musicians. They had their own world, apart from the rest of the people. This was the other half of the man, the dreamer who made music and put words to it. His poems had a rhythm like music, so she should have known. His reddish hair was falling over his forehead, but he didn't know it. He was writing a word, touching a key.

He was having a problem with that passage, yet it seemed to her that the answer was in the notes he'd already written. She couldn't have expressed it in notes or words, but if she had a guitar in her arms she thought she could play the music. He didn't seem to notice as she crossed the room. It wasn't her guitar, but it was the same type. Her fingers found the notes softly, the sound strengthening, following his lead, the music filling and flowing between them.

As the sounds of the guitar faded, the song grew, renewed, from Lyle's synthesiser. George found her fingers improvising, the volume swelling, her own voice humming wordless sounds that had to fit with the rhythm and the mood.

The music faded slowly, leaving its heat behind. She let her fingers go lax on the guitar strings.

His eyes were on her, a disturbing light in their depths that might almost be anger. She was suddenly and unexpectedly frightened of him.

'I'm sorry,' she began, but he shook his head, denying anger. She strummed a chord, picking up the melody of his tune. The sound of music from her fingers made her comfortable, gave her confidence. 'Lyle, you should try selling that song. It's terrific!'

'Should I?' His eyes sparkled quiet laughter.

She frowned at his equipment, realising, 'This is obviously a professional set-up.'

'I'm trying,' he said simply. He jotted something on the notebook in front of him. 'I liked that echo you put in, repeating the melody—I was having a hell of a time with that passage.'

He pushed an impatient hand through his unruly hair, saw her watching.

'Need a haircut,' he mumbled.

She was surprised to realise that he was embarrassed. He always seemed so strong and confident. Even in his concern over Robin, he seemed to know instinctively what to do.

His discomfort disarmed her. Impulsively, she said, 'I'll cut it, if you like.'

He smiled then. 'Sounds like a gift from heaven.'

Her smile caught from his. She'd been frightened, coming down here after the scene in the bedroom, but it was all right. He was going to let her pretend it had never happened. She said gaily, 'You're taking a chance, you know. I'm no expert, but Jenny did let me cut hers.'

His fingers brought the synthesiser to life again. 'Could you cut it tomorrow?'

'Tomorrow,' she agreed as the music swelled, flowing over them both. This time the rhythm was completed, the hesitation gone as Lyle filled in the notes she had supplied.

'I think I'm getting it.' He threw a switch, then held out a piece of paper for her to take. 'Here's the music—a bit rough, but would you try it for me? I'd like to hear it with just the guitar. And could I talk you into singing the words? You do have a singing voice, don't you? You were humming like a pro.'

She took the paper from his hands, wishing she didn't have to say, 'I don't read music very well. I just learned to play by ear.'

His fingers brushed soft curls back from her face as
he wondered why she should apologise for anything. He
was watching her, seeming to see something reassuring
in her eyes. 'Feeling better now?' he murmured, nodding
in answer to his own question. 'Play the music as best
you can remember it, would you? I'd like to hear it.
Then perhaps I'll teach you to read music. It's certainly
time you learned. I—what's wrong?'

She blinked away a vivid memory of Scott towering
over her in a West End coffee house, his eyes filled with
the quiet anger that hurt so much. He had stared at her
as the music faded away, then there had been the uncomfortable silence of the others, as if they'd known he
shouldn't have found her here. She had scrambled to her
feet.

'I'm sorry, Scott! I'm late again, aren't I? I'm sorry!'

'Georgina, don't you think it's time you grew up, time
to stop playing about like a teenager? It's time you
learned a sense of responsibility.'

'George?' Lyle's voice was sharp. She stared down at
the guitar in her arms, wishing she'd done more to be
the wife she should have been. Scott had asked so little,
and she'd seemed to have such trouble giving it.

'George?'

She met Lyle's eyes, saw the question in his fade as if
she had answered it without words. He knew. She felt
ashamed, and confused, without understanding the
reason for either emotion.

'Will you sing my song, George? I'd like to hear it.'

She looked down at the paper. He was making this
too easy. He should be angry. Upstairs, in his arms, she'd
done the unforgivable. And she was still doing it, remembering Scott and letting Lyle see her thoughts. What
kind of a woman was she?

He played the tune softly for her, as if he knew that
she needed no more than a reminder to fix the notes and
the rhythm in her mind.

She fled her discomfort, took refuge in the music. The words were soft and haunting, fitting for the notes that her fingers coaxed from the guitar. It was a song of love and healing. As she sang it, George could see Robin growing strong and confident until she walked away from her father to a love and a life of her own.

'Robin's song,' she said softly as the music faded.

'Yes,' he agreed quietly.

She picked out the melody again, low and haunting. 'It could be a hit,' she said warmly, humming the refrain. 'You should——' She broke off at the hint of laughter in his eyes. 'No, you already have, haven't you?'

He shook his head. 'I'm trying, George. Breaking into the music industry isn't easy. I've had a few songs picked up, but no hit songs yet.'

She picked out a tune on the guitar, notes she remembered hearing once on one of the radio stations. 'It's yours, isn't it? I heard it on the radio in Vancouver.' She saw the pleasure in his eyes and was glad she'd put it there.

'I didn't know it had made it to the airwaves, though. Was Annie Carson the singer?'

'I think so. Yes.'

He nodded, adjusting the dials, then switching the synthesiser off. 'I think Annie did all right with it, but it didn't make the top ten or anything like that. George, why didn't you tell me you were a guitar-playing lady with a voice?'

She shrugged self-consciously. 'I just play at it, but you—Lyle, what are you doing stuck out on a lighthouse in the middle of the Pacific?'

'The edge of the Pacific,' he corrected.

She frowned at him sternly, angry at the waste of his talent. How could he promote his songs from here? He had to get closer to the music world, mix with the people who could be singing his songs. 'Don't joke about it. I don't understand why you're making music like that, and living in a place like this! Your songs are very distinctive. They have that something that——' She waved an expressive arm. He followed her gesture with his eyes.

'Is it so bad here?' he asked curiously. He shuffled his papers together and placed them carefully in the top drawer of the desk. 'I rather like the house. It's got——'

'It's not the house,' she retorted angrily. 'It's the island! Five hundred feet of rock and grass!'

'Six hundred feet!' He was angry, too. 'And a fabulous ocean view!'

She shrugged impatiently, standing up and pacing restlessly. Just talking about the smallness of his island made her feel stifled, trapped. 'Five hundred or six hundred, it's too small! Don't you think you should be out in the world, instead of hiding out here, out of contact?'

'George!' His voice dropped, yet somehow became more harsh. 'Since you know nothing about the circumstances, don't you think you should stop trying to make me angry by telling me how to live my life?'

'I——' She realised suddenly that somehow her attack was hurting him.

He moved sharply. She could hear his breathing, shallow and disturbed, but his voice was carefully casual as he said, 'We both need some fresh air. Come on, let's get outside. Put on some shoes and socks while I check on Robin, then we'll go for a walk.'

She was glad to escape the disturbed emotional atmosphere that had grown in the music-room.

Outside, the night air was cool and salty, the fog engulfing the far end of the island. Lyle took George's hand as they walked down the outside stairs. The wind had stopped. She should pull her hand away. But it was dark. He knew the way, and she didn't. Her fingers curled around his.

At the front of the house he led her towards a steep path that twisted down to a small beach. Their silence was easy and companionable. Where had the anger gone?

'Can you climb?' he asked, his hand holding hers tightly, as if he would keep her safe against the night.

'I think so.' She wanted the exertion, the feeling of movement to get her away from too much emotion. She flexed the muscles of her thigh, said, 'Of course I can.'

He laughed softly, leading her towards the path, asking whimsically, 'What's the longest you've ever stayed in bed?'

She had to hang on to his hand going down the steep path. She couldn't see the ground below her feet. With anyone else she might have felt nervous. With Lyle it was somehow impossible to be uneasy.

She wondered if they could forget what had happened tonight. They could be friends then, like brother and sister.

'The longest I've been sick, you mean?'

'Mm-hmm.'

It was nice, walking together, feeling his warm, rough hand around hers. If they were friends—there weren't many friends that lasted for ever, but Lyle would. He had come close to something deep inside her. Someone she could always come back to. She'd have two people then. Lyle and Jenny.

She said, 'I don't usually get sick. This shipwreck. Chicken-pox when I was a kid. And last year I was in hospital for a few days.'

He stepped on to the sand, turned back and closed his hands securely around her waist to swing her down the last couple of feet. His hands remained warm against her as he stared down in the misty darkness. 'What happened?'

She felt so secure, so safe. Was this unfair? Was she teasing him by standing in his arms? 'My cousin and I

were on the west coast of the Queen Charlotte Islands—
sailing—and I had a big feed of clams.'

'Red tide?' He either saw or felt the motion of her
nod of assent. 'You were lucky to survive it.' He sounded
frightened.

'Jake came,' she explained, wanting to reassure him.
'He came just in time and flew Jenny and I into Queen
Charlotte.'

'Who's Jake?' Then he remembered, 'Jenny's
husband? Your cousin's husband?' His arm slipped up
over her shoulder as he turned her and started them
walking over the sand.

There was nothing sexual in the feel of his arm on her
shoulder. Earlier he'd wanted her, but that could have
been just a natural male reaction to a scantily dressed
woman in his arms.

That was it, of course. It had happened, and it was
over now. So she could relax, let herself enjoy this. What
had they been talking about? Oh, yes—Jake and Jenny.

'Yes—well, they weren't married then. She was
running away from him, and he was firmly in pursuit.
They're married now, and very happy—I didn't know
this beach was here. Why didn't I see it from my
window?'

'It's covered by the water at high tide.' She shivered.
He drew her closer. 'Are you dressed warmly enough?'

'It was just that bit of wind.' Funny. She'd never been
friends with a man like this before. Was it like this having
a brother who was close?

'Tell me about Jenny.'

She did, her voice warm with her affection for her
cousin as she told Jenny and Jake's love story.

Then she found herself telling Lyle about their
childhood, the escapades she and Jenny had got into.

'It was me,' she told him with a laugh. 'I was always
in trouble, always refusing to stay where I should be, to

do what was expected of me. My mother was always upset.'

Lyle had moved them to a low rock where he could lean and hold her in his arms, giving her his warmth. 'What about your father?'

She drew away. She didn't often think about her father. Not any more. It was so long ago, and it hurt remembering that he was gone.

'I remember when I was—oh, about ten, I guess, Jenny and I were out in the dinghy. We weren't supposed to, but I'd talked her into it and we were out on the water. The wind came up and I was scared. I had to pretend to Jenny that I wasn't afraid, that it was all right. I was older, and she'd come only because I did. But inside I wasn't sure we'd make it back. We did—just barely! When we landed on the beach, my father was there, striding over the sand towards us. He looked ten feet tall, and furious.'

'What did he do?' Lyle's hand rubbed along her arm, absently caressing through the thick Mackinaw he'd made her put on.

She shivered, but it was only a remembered cold. 'He took us home. I was terrified of what he'd say, but he didn't say a word. I was trembling, afraid, and he bundled me out of the car and said, "Get to bed!" and that was the end of it...but I knew better than to take the dinghy out alone again.'

The slow surf crawled over the sand, its sound warm in the darkness. Lyle's arms were close around her.

'He died when I was thirteen.'

Lyle's lips found her cheek. 'That's a bad age to lose someone who means so much.'

She'd never said this to anyone, but now she admitted, 'I thought the world had ended. I shouldn't have. There was my mother, and Jenny moved in with us when her parents went overseas, so I wasn't alone. But I was pretending, going through the motions, until——'

A sea bird cried and George shivered.

'Until you met Scott?'

'Yes,' she whispered. Scott. Suddenly it was all welling inside her, and she had to talk, to let it out. 'I was seventeen, and ... he was there. I couldn't believe that he wanted me, that it was really me. It was like coming to life, having someone of my own, being in love and——'

She broke off, shuddering, remembering her awakening earlier that night. Her voice was so low he had to bend closer to hear the words. 'I'm sorry, Lyle. I—God! It was unforgivable, but I need him so badly! I can't——'

She pulled away, pulled the knowledge of the cold closer, as if it brought strength. She seemed to have no control over her emotions any more. Love and loneliness and fear and need—they swept through her of their own volition. She was suddenly afraid of what she might do or say next.

'I think you should leave me here alone,' she said harshly. 'I don't know what's gotten into me tonight, but I—I've really said enough—done enough for one night.'

She walked a few steps away, needing to be alone, but somehow knowing he wouldn't leave her there. She took a deep, ragged breath, wishing for sunshine and cold wind, for numbness, distance from her own emotions.

Lyle's quiet voice hit her like a slap of the cold water she had wanted. 'It's time you woke up and started looking around yourself, George.'

She jerked around, welcoming the sensation of anger. It wasn't his pain or his business. He'd no place intruding, handing out words of wisdom.

'What's that supposed to mean?' she asked harshly. 'I'm awake. I've got eyes.'

He stepped closer, his voice dropped as hers rose, holding her attention against her will. 'You're so busy feeling sorry for yourself, grieving, that you've no time left to live life, to really take part in it.'

She gasped, her hands forming fists. 'What do you think I'm doing, crawling into a corner? I'm out sailing, seeing the world. I'm not sitting at home, hiding from life.'

'No,' he agreed slowly, as if he saw everything she had hidden from the rest of the world. She wished she hadn't let herself feel close to him, because now he was turning their intimacy against her, accusing. 'You're not hiding, you're running from life. You've lost your husband, your father. You're sorry for yourself. You're holding on to your grief, telling yourself that George is a brave girl because she pretends she's happy when she's really miserable.'

She hugged herself, wanting to turn away, but somehow frozen by the quiet certainty of his voice. 'And just what do you think I should be doing?' she asked with low bitterness.

He came close, framed her face with his hands. Even in the dark she felt her eyes trapped by the intensity of his. 'Let him go. He's gone, George... You loved him, and he loved you. It's over now. You're left with the memories... only the memories. It's time you put the memories where they belong, in the past, and got involved in life again.'

'I am involved,' she denied weakly.

'Are you?' His thumbs kneaded her cheekbones softly, demanding, 'Who is in your life, George? There's no one, is there? You're moving through the world, alone, avoiding even the people who might once have been close to you.'

She shook her head in a weak denial, but he wouldn't stop. 'Why wasn't there anyone to call when you landed up here, George? Who's keeping track of your journey? Where are your family, your friends?'

She found the strength to pull away from those tender hands. Her voice was tight. 'I have friends.'

She could see his head move in denial, disbelief. 'Friends, but none that have a claim on you. You move on before they can get close.'

It was true. She found her head bending in assent. There was only Jenny, and even Jenny she kept at a distance.

CHAPTER FIVE

THE next morning George got up early, belted Lyle's dressing-gown tightly around her and went into the bathroom for her shower. Ever since the shipwreck she'd been drifting, lost on a tide of feelings and reactions. It was time for her to get back control of her own life. She made an action plan as the water pounded down on her. First, pin down Lyle about getting transportation off this island.

Lyle. His eyes and his hands and the music. Robin and the dog and——

Saying goodbye.

Perhaps she could come back to visit. Later, when she had herself in control again.

First she had to leave. To do that, she needed transportation. Transportation first. Then—she and Robin could go for a walk, exploring the intertidal zone. Robin would like that. If the sun shone, perhaps Robin could do her school lessons on the lawn.

Later...later she would cut Lyle's hair. Not too short, she decided as her fingers worked shampoo into a lather in her own hair. She wouldn't want to cut away the locks that waved across his forehead.

What would it feel like to run her fingers through that softly waving hair, feeling—— Damn!

She scrubbed harder at her scalp, tensing against the warm sensations that were flooding under her skin. Talk about men having a one-track mind! She couldn't seem to stop herself from thinking about Lyle's hair, his hands, or the man himself. This was some kind of belated reaction to her widowhood, because no man had been able to touch her since Scott died.

Scott. This morning his image floated across her mind like a memory, lacking substance.

Soaped and rinsed, she dried her body roughly with the towel, tried to stop thinking about everything except leaving.

Lyle's hair. A walk with Robin. Should she cook dinner for them tonight? Not that she was a gourmet cook, but then, neither was Lyle from the evidence she'd seen. What else? Would Lyle let her into his music-room again, to play his guitar and sing his songs? Or even just to listen?

Transportation—that was the first thing, the most important. Not music. Not Lyle.

The dresser drawer contained more clothes. She put her own jeans on, topped with an unfamiliar sweatshirt that asked, 'Where the heck is Kitimat, BC?' The shirt was loose enough that she could leave her bra off without it showing. She was far too sore to put it on again. Where was Kitimat, anyway? And whose shirt was this? Dorothy's, perhaps?

The kitchen was filled with warmth and noise. Lyle was at the stove, turning strips of bacon in a big cast-iron frying-pan. Russ was sitting astride a kitchen chair turned backwards. Robin was setting the table.

Russ tilted the chair, asking Lyle, 'What should I do about number two generator?'

Lyle neatly laid two more strips of bacon in the pan. 'Shut it down and put number one on. We'll take a look at it later this morning. If we can't see what the problem is, I'll send in a message tonight to the district manager. How many eggs, Russ?'

Robin spotted George, and put down a plate with a bang and a smile. 'Are you going to eat with us? Daddy said you might want to get up this morning!'

Lyle said, 'You're looking nice this morning,' and she found herself returning his warm smile as she pushed her hands into the pockets of her jeans.

'I thought it was time I got up for my meals. Can I help set the table?'

His eyes flashed from warmth to a deep intensity that reminded her of the night before, of his hands stroking her heated skin. She flushed and turned quickly to Robin.

Businesslike, the little girl said, 'We need another plate. And jam for the toast. You set the plates and I'll get the jam.' She limped quickly towards the pantry, Tom following close behind her. The cat got stopped by the kitchen door as Robin closed it behind her, so sheared off and sniffed hopefully around Lyle's ankles.

'Forget it, Tom!' Lyle said sternly. 'I'm not in the mood to drop any scraps for you. Did you sleep well, George?'

'Fine.' She kept her eyes on the plates she was setting. She wanted to walk over to him and touch him, to say hello with more than her voice.

Transportation, she reminded herself.

Russ shifted, his chair squeaking on the floor. 'It's hard to believe Lyle fished you out of the water last week. We both thought you were dead when you came out.'

Russ's eyes were a friendly grey. George found herself grinning and admitting, 'Fool that I was, sailing your waters in a March storm! I'm glad you found me.'

'Lyle did the finding,' said Russ easily, tossing back an unruly lock of hair. They looked so much alike, these two brothers. George smiled as Lyle unobtrusively slipped a piece of bacon to the cat.

Russ said, 'He woke me up and dragged me down to the north end, determined there was a shipwreck out there.'

'It was the dog,' Lyle explained. 'Scruff was spooky, wouldn't let me rest.'

'I've got to thank Scruff, then.' She stared at the table and took a deep breath. 'Because I'm all right now, and I wouldn't have been. But today——'

'A haircut?' Lyle reminded her softly. 'You promised me a haircut.'

Russ's chair attacked the tile again as he jerked to attention. 'You're going to give Lyle a haircut? You cut hair? Would you do mine? Dorothy—my wife—usually does it, but—I'd kind of like to be looking at least respectable when I next see her.'

Lyle lifted several pieces of bacon out of the pan, said repressively, 'She isn't running a barber shop!'

George said, 'I don't mind. I'll cut it—if you want to take your chances.' That was what she needed. Something practical and physical to do. 'But I'll need scissors. I don't have my barber shears with me.'

Russ pushed his chair aside. 'I'll get Dorothy's. Won't be a minute!'

'And after the haircuts,' George said determinedly, 'I think it's time I worked out a way to get back to the mainland. I'm better, and——'

'Chopper,' said Russ, pausing half-way through the doorway. 'You can hitch a ride with me on Wednesday.'

Lyle brought the plate of bacon across to the table as Russ's boots pounded down the outside stairs.

'Chopper?' she asked the back of Lyle's reddish-blond head. Was he avoiding looking at her?

'Helicopter.' Lyle walked back to the stove, turned the eggs in a second frying-pan. Yes, he was deliberately avoiding her eyes. 'How many eggs, honey?'

'Honey? I'm not——'

'How many?' he repeated with a grin, his eyes teasing her now.

'I'm not your honey!'

Friends! They were only friends. She jerked down on the Kitimat shirt. 'I—two eggs, please. When is the helicopter coming? Why?' Did friends call each other *honey*?

Lyle cracked two eggs into the frying-pan. 'Russ goes on holidays Wednesday. The chopper is scheduled to pick him up some time Wednesday and take him into Prince Rupert.'

'Wednesday? And I could go on it?' She turned to look out of the window, as if she could see Prince Rupert in the distance. 'And today—what's today?'

'Sunday,' he said abruptly.

'Why didn't you tell me before? When I asked you if I could get a seaplane? You must have known then. Why didn't you tell me?' She moved around the table to conceal her rapid breathing. The answer was there in his eyes, and it wasn't the answer she wanted. How could he be a friend, someone she could turn to, if he felt like that about her?

He said softly, 'Why do you think, stray lady? I'm in no hurry to see you leave.'

She adjusted a plate that didn't need moving. 'I don't belong here. It's time for me to go.' She could never come back. She'd been crazy, pretending she could. 'I'm better now.'

'Are you?'

He was standing on the other side of the room, holding her still with those deep blue eyes. 'Where will you go, honey? Don't you think you'd rather stay here for a while?'

She broke contact, looked away. He wanted too much from her. 'There's nothing to keep me here,' she said with a hint of desperation. 'Wednesday, you said. Wednesday, I'll hitch a ride on the helicopter. Can—could you please arrange it?'

'I can arrange it,' he said flatly. 'Your eggs are ready.'

The kitchen door snapped shut with a bang. Lyle and George both swung towards the door to see Robin standing with the jam in her hands. She was staring at George with a stricken look on her face.

'You're not going?' she whispered. 'George? Are you really leaving us?'

Lyle and his daughter. They were both determined to make it hard for her to go.

'I can't stay for ever, Robin. I have to go some time.'

Lyle said, 'George has people waiting for her. Her own people. They need her back.'

It wasn't true. Lyle's eyes challenged her to deny it, but thankfully Robin had no way of knowing. She was staring at George, shaking her head in protest as Lyle reached her and placed a gentle hand on her shoulder. 'George isn't ours, honey,' he said softly. 'We can't keep her.' His voice became casual, lighter. 'Is that the strawberry jam? How about getting some marmalade as well? I'm pretty sure there's a jar left in the pantry.'

When Robin was gone, he said, 'She hasn't formed a relationship with any woman since her mother left and—well, she's going to have trouble accepting that you're going away.'

'This isn't a relationship,' she said desperately, talking about more than Robin. 'I'm sorry, but I—it's only been a few days. It can't really mean anything.'

'Time has nothing to do with it. She started loving you before you ever opened your eyes. The sea brought you to us—cold and battered and——'

She turned away impatiently. She was done with remembering. She scoffed, 'A stray? Is that how you both think of me? You and your daughter, you're two of a kind! You think everyone who has a hurt is yours to take in and——'

'And love?'

'No!' She hadn't meant to shout. She got her voice under control, said, 'I have to go some time.'

She welcomed the sound of Russ running back up the outside stairs. 'Scissors!' he announced, bursting through the kitchen doorway. 'I've found them!'

'I'll do your hair after breakfast,' she offered.

'It'll have to wait,' said Lyle. Robin came back with another jar. He held a chair for her to sit down. 'Russ and I have a generator to service this morning.'

'Then I'll explore.' Outside, in the wind and spray, she'd quickly get herself back to normal. 'Could you take me around the island, Robin?'

Robin wasn't answering, wasn't meeting George's eyes. She sat silently at the table, pushing her food around.

'I switched over the generator,' said Russ to his brother.

George leapt at a subject that had no emotional content. 'What's wrong with the generator?'

Russ began to outline the problem in technical terms that she couldn't begin to understand. At first she listened, but the words got longer. It began to seem as if Russ was determined to share all his knowledge with her. She met Lyle's eyes and they both started to laugh. Russ stopped explaining in mid-jargon.

'What's wrong?'

Lyle chuckled. 'She didn't want a course in diesels, Russ. What he's trying to say, George, is that it isn't running evenly.'

Robin giggled and said, 'It's sick, Uncle Russ,' and only giggled louder when her uncle glared at her. 'We need an engine doctor.'

Russ shrugged with good nature and growled, 'Serves me right for taking a job under my big brother. Never get taken seriously. Say, George, where did you get that shirt?'

She looked down at it. 'It was in the drawer in my—in the room I'm sleeping in. I thought maybe it was your wife's. I've been wondering ever since I put it on just where the heck Kitimat is.'

Lyle's smile had turned to a frown. He picked up some egg with his fork. 'It's south of Prince Rupert, on one of the inland channels. There's an aluminium smelter there and a town of ten to fifteen thousand people.'

'Is it all right if I wear the shirt?' She squirmed uncomfortably under Lyle's gaze. 'It was in the drawer with my jeans and——'

Robin said, 'I put it there, Daddy. Remember the things Cynthia left behind? I thought George could use 'em, 'cause Cynthia never came back.'

Who was Cynthia?

Lyle shrugged and picked up the plate of bacon. 'You having some of this bacon, Russ?'

Suddenly she knew. Cynthia must have been Lyle's lover.

'Cynthia?' repeated Russ slowly. He ignored, or didn't see, the quelling glance his brother gave him. 'Have you heard from Cynthia lately? You haven't mentioned her in——' He broke off and explained to George, 'Cynthia lived here with Lyle for—how long, Lyle? She was here when I arrived a year ago, but she left shortly——'

'Shut up, Russ!'

His hand stopped in mid-air, a piece of bacon hanging from his fork precariously. 'Oh,' Russ said on a note of discovery, looking from Lyle to George. 'Sorry, Lyle. I——'

Robin leaned towards George and whispered loudly, 'Cynthia wasn't really very nice. I didn't like her much.'

Lyle threw down his fork. 'I don't believe this!' he muttered to no one in particular. He glared at George, then said tightly, 'For your information, Cynthia McLeod——'

'I didn't ask, and it's really none of my business.' Of course she didn't care about his affairs. She couldn't seem to avoid looking at him, and she hoped she didn't look as if she cared who he slept with. 'I—Robin, are you finished eating? Why don't we go out now and you can show me the island?'

She stood up abruptly, leaving the half-eaten breakfast, saying brightly, 'You two go ahead and do your mechanical magic with the generator. Robin and I will clean up these dishes after we have our walk.'

Scruff followed George and Robin when they went to get ready, leaving the kitchen silent with only the two men at the table.

'Lyle?' said Russ tentatively after a moment.

Lyle stared at his food. He loved his family but, by God, they surely could put their foot in it! Courting George was going to be tricky enough, without Russ throwing spanners in his path. And Cynthia, for God's sake!

'Sorry, man. I had no idea that you——'

'Russ, would you please shut up?'

She wanted to leave. Well, why not? Once she was gone, he could forget her, get his life back to normal.

George was standing in the bedroom she had come to think of as hers, stripping off the Kitimat sweatshirt while Robin stood by the door watching her.

'I don't think Daddy liked her very much,' volunteered Robin.

'That's his affair,' said George, pulling on another shirt from the next drawer. 'Whose is this?'

'Uncle Russ brought it over. It's Aunt Dorothy's.'

She pulled the blue shirt over her head and turned to Robin. Affairs. Well, of course he'd had affairs. His wife was gone, apparently years ago. He was a very attractive man, and it was only natural that there were women. It certainly didn't matter to George Dobson how many women he had, how many affairs.

Cynthia had lived here. Had she used this room? No, of course not. She would have shared the room across the hallway. She and Lyle——

'He likes you a lot more than Cynthia,' Robin said. 'And so do I.'

George pulled on a sweater over the blue shirt. It was big. Lyle's? She didn't care who he liked. His wife had come and gone. This Cynthia had come and gone. Right now he wanted George, but by next year he'd be thinking

about someone else. It didn't matter. She wasn't in the
market for a man, for heaven's sake!

She followed Robin down to the helicopter pad. Despite her limp, Robin seemed agile enough when she
walked over the rocks beyond the helicopter pad.

'The seagulls fill this part in the summer,' she told
George. 'And in the winter the storms come and when
you look down here it's all white spray. Noisy and—oh,
George! You should see it in the winter.'

'Tell me,' George invited.

The tide was out, making the island much larger. They
walked back by the beach, both limping slightly on the
gravel, but climbing over the logs that appeared in their
path without hesitation.

Winter on Green Island.

'Noisy,' said Robin. 'The wind comes and it's noisy
for weeks. Draughts bang in the chimneys. Daddy puts
up ropes 'tween the buildings and we can't go out without
hanging on to 'em. The wind's fierce! Daddy takes me
out sometimes, just in the shelter of the buildings, lets
me watch the waves just explode over the island! White
and fog and noise all over!'

What kind of music did Lyle write when the winter
storms raged? Wasn't he lonely in the long winter nights?

Robin straddled a log, facing George, rubbing her leg
absently. 'George, are you gonna be in Vancouver in
May?'

George found herself moving, drawing the girl closer
with an arm around her shoulders. She looked so vulnerable. 'I'm not sure where I'll be in May,' she admitted, feeling strangely depressed by the thought. 'Why?
Are you going to be in Vancouver then?'

Robin's long hair obscured her face as she nodded.
'They're doin' my leg again. In the General Hospital.'

'Would you like me to visit you?' Would Lyle stay at
the Holiday Inn again? May in Vancouver. Seeing Lyle
and Robin again.

'It's the last time they'll cut my leg open,' said Robin.

'I'll be there,' George promised, and Robin smiled.

Well, why not? By May she would surely be over this temporary insanity.

What would it feel like if Robin were hers—hers and Lyle's?

He had intended to avoid George for the rest of the day but, after he had finished working on the generator, Lyle found himself washing up, then going outside to find Robin and George.

He found them on the beach, sitting together on a big log. They were close together, Robin's long hair blowing across George's chest with an intimacy he wished he could share. George's short hair was tossed wildly around her face, a turbulent riot of silvery blonde. She was looking down at Robin with a tenderness that caught his throat.

'Daddy!' Robin had seen him, her quiet face lighting up as she scrambled off the log and flung herself into his arms, giving him a hearty kiss.

'Nice,' he said, laughing, giving her a hug before she slipped out of his arms. George hadn't moved from her perch on the log, but she was watching. He recognised the wistful look in her eyes as one he had seen in Robin's when she was feeling lonely and in need of loving. It was a look he couldn't resist. 'What about you?' he asked softly.

'Me?' Her hands rubbed along her thighs. He wished she weren't so nervous of him.

She'd changed out of the Kitimat shirt. He found himself taking a sharp pleasure in the knowledge that she'd worn one of his sweaters. He was getting so obsessed by this woman, to the extent that he'd probably find himself taking that sweater to bed with him when she was gone, just to pretend she was near.

'Don't I get a kiss from you, too?' he asked softly.

'Yes,' Robin agreed eagerly. 'Give Daddy a kiss. He needs lots of kisses.'

Her tongue circled her lips nervously. Her voice was husky. She wanted to run, but instead she asked, 'Why? Why should I?'

He answered simply, 'Because I want you to,' and watched her eyes widen. His heart thundered as he saw her lips part, as if anticipating his kiss.

He held out a hand for her as she started to slip down from the log. She drew back. 'Do you always get what you want?'

'Not always.' He thought he would drown in her eyes. Then her hand was in his and he pulled her towards him. 'I'm hoping I will this time. Are you going to kiss me, honey?'

She shook her head, slipping down to the gravel of the beach, coming to rest trapped between the log and Lyle. He could smell the enticing scent of her, see the quick rise and fall of her breasts. Her nipples hardened as he watched, and he sucked in a breath at the sight of them thrusting. He wanted badly to pull her into his arms.

'Afraid?' he asked gently. Then, on an inspiration, he challenged softly, 'I dare you.'

Her eyes sparkled with his challenge, then suddenly she was close, not quite touching her body to his as she stood on tiptoe. Her lips brushed his in a brief caress, drawing away quickly as he started to respond. His hands found her hips as she drew away.

She lost her balance, falling against him. He gasped as her softness pressed into him.

'Let me go!' she said sharply, but her arms were still against him, her hands spread over his chest.

'Why would I want to do that? I want a real kiss,' he growled, drawn like a magnet to her parted lips, praying she wouldn't push him away.

She tasted like honey, sweet and addictive, her lips moving under his, her mouth firming in response as his tongue explored. His hands slipped up over the sweater, feeling the curve of her back as he drew her against him, the soft pressure of her breasts pressed against his chest.

'George,' he groaned softly, dropping his lips to the softness of her throat, feeling her shudder in response to his kisses.

Then the gravel crunched under Robin's feet and Lyle remembered where he was, his daughter standing watching avidly. He took a ragged breath and drew his lips away from George's.

Her eyes were closed. She opened them slowly, her gaze unfocused for a moment. Then her head came up and he saw, for just an instant, her silent admission of desire. If they had been alone...

'Will you sing for me tonight?' he asked. He couldn't ask for any of the other things he wanted from her: her body against his, warm and welcoming, her lips, her touch, her love.

He was learning to need so much from her—her laughter and her singing, her quick fiery spirit whenever she thought her independence might be threatened. 'You will sing for me tonight, won't you?'

She met his eyes. They were dark and narrowed, seemed to be asking so much more than the words he spoke. She felt a sudden, painful need to say yes, to agree to anything this man wanted of her. He would touch her and hold her, drawing her back into his arms and she could stay for ever.

For ever. Nothing lasted for ever.

She slipped quickly out from between the man and the log. 'Yes,' she said. Then, 'Yes,' again, trying to get the husky invitation out of her voice. 'I'll sing,' she added, suddenly afraid he might have mistaken her meaning.

'Good,' he said, but he wasn't smiling.

'Do you still want that haircut?'

Cutting his hair was harder than she had expected. She made him shampoo it first, then sat him on a chair in the kitchen, a towel wrapped around his neck. The water slid through as she combed his hair, then her fingers lifted and separated and the scissors snipped, but she had to work to keep her hands from trembling, to keep her fingers from exploring the contours of his scalp under the damp, waving hair.

Robin watched for a few minutes, until Lyle said firmly, 'School!' Then they were alone in the kitchen. George stood behind Lyle as she snipped. He couldn't see her face and she didn't have to try to wear a mask.

She could enjoy the intimacy of his hair in her hands, knowing he couldn't see her pleasure.

'Want to go fishing this afternoon?' he asked after a long silence.

She let a damp curl wrap itself around her finger before she carefully snipped it shorter. 'Fishing? From shore?'

'No, from a boat.' The curl pulled out of her fingers as his head moved.

What would he do if she moved around to the front of him and sat down in his lap? Would his arms go around her as her hands reached up into that softly waving hair?

'Are you afraid?' he asked softly.

'What?' She sucked in a deep breath. He couldn't see her face, but her fingers might have transmitted her wanton thoughts. 'What do you mean? Afraid of what?'

'Afraid of the water. Of going out in a boat.'

'Oh—no, I don't think so.' She separated a section of his hair with her comb. He had asked her to cut his hair short, but she was leaving enough of the curl to run her fingers through.

Oh, lord! Was she actually considering having an affair with him? She mustn't! He was too dangerous, too easily able to stir all kinds of needs that could never be satisfied.

She talked nervously, filling the silence. 'I'm not afraid of the water. I suppose I should be, after *Lady Harriet* going down, but—sit still, please, Lyle. You're going to have a mess on your head if you don't quit jerking around!'

He caught her hand. Could he feel her pulse thundering under his fingers? She licked her lips. The fingers of her entrapped hand clenched on the scissors. Lyle's thumb rubbed across the inside of her wrist, then he reached across with his other hand and took the scissors from her.

'If it isn't the water you're afraid of,' he said slowly, his thumb caressing the inner surface of her wrist, 'then I think it must be me.'

She couldn't seem to drag her eyes away from his, couldn't make herself laugh or change the subject. How could she deny it when her heart was pounding, when she desperately wanted him to pull her closer and kiss her again? And all the while she was terribly afraid that he might actually do that, take her and entrap her for ever.

'Yes, it's you.' She couldn't break his gaze, but she found the strength to pull her hand away from his grip. 'Could I have the scissors back? I'll finish your hair. Then I'll cut Russ's.'

'And then?' he demanded softly, laughter and something else in his eyes.

'And then you can take us fishing,' she evaded.

His eyes flashed. 'George, do you always pull away when a man gets close?'

'Always,' she said firmly, taking the scissors back.

Look what happened when a man got too close. Scott. And her father.

She took refuge in chatter. 'And especially men named Lyle. Now be quiet, or I'll jab you with these scissors.'

He subsided, but he was smiling. She had the uncomfortable feeling that if they were counting points, Lyle was winning.

CHAPTER SIX

GEORGE caught a small flounder. Robin caught a halibut that was too big for her to reel in on her own, so Lyle took over.

Lyle caught nothing. George thought he wasn't trying, but he seemed to enjoy leaning back and watching them.

She was enjoying it, too. There was a warm simplicity in their spending time together in a small boat, alone on the water. The wind was light, making only small waves that rocked the boat gently.

George felt good. Warm and excited and relaxed. She couldn't remember feeling quite like this before.

When they tired of fishing, Lyle opened up the engine and the small boat rose up and raced across the open water towards Dundas Island two miles away.

George thought she might use the insurance money from *Lady Harriet* to buy a speedboat. Something fast and white, with lots of power. She had an absurd desire to trap this feeling, to keep it for ever.

'Do you use your seaplane a lot out here?' she asked.

'In the summer, yes.' He had to shout over the sound of the engine to make her hear. 'Stick around a while and I'll show you something of this country. If you stay, I could arrange to have my plane delivered next week. It's in Prince Rupert right now. I store it there for the winter, 'til the spring storms are over.'

Flying with Lyle. High over these islands, looking down on the world. They'd be observers, together in their world and untouched by anything in the world below.

Oh, lord! More fantasies. As if anyone could be untouched. Sharing like that was asking for pain, for loss.

She looked away, narrowed her eyes to keep out the wind and stared off at the horizon. 'I have to go on Wednesday!' She let the wind carry her words back. 'I have to see my insurance agent, and——' She shrugged, an indication of numerous chores and duties she must do.

Robin had curled up beside Lyle, her eyes closed and her mouth slightly open as she slept.

The boat slowed suddenly, settling down in its own wake, rocking as they came to a silent stop with water all around.

'You could come back,' he said carefully.

The affinity between her and Lyle could never stop at mere friendship. Whenever they came close emotionally, she could feel the strength of the pull. If she got too close, she would never be free.

She shook her head silently, refusing to look at him, but his words kept echoing. She could come back. She didn't have to go.

She couldn't lay herself open like that again. She'd be caught, stuck, committed. Terrified, she pushed away the temptation to let Lyle draw her closer.

She helped Robin with her English assignment, then insisted on making supper for them all. She cooked the fish, making English-style fish and chips, something she knew she wasn't likely to make a mess of.

When evening came, she tucked Robin into bed while Lyle gave the weather report, then she slipped away as Lyle came into the girl's bedroom.

She went silently down to the room in the basement, closing the door behind her. While Lyle said goodnight to Robin, she had this private room to herself.

She tuned his guitar, strumming softly, blanking her mind with the sounds she was creating.

With her eyes half closed, the music came from wherever it was that music lived. She felt the peace sweeping over her, then the feeling of power, as if she could do anything, be anything she wanted.

She didn't hear him come in.

The music was all around her. She half opened her eyes, singing for someone who wasn't there, and she saw a man's tall shape beside her, towering over her.

Fear and guilt surged through her.

'What's wrong?' he asked.

'Nothing,' she said, but her voice was shaking. Her eyes dropped to the guitar. Her fingers started to move again.

'When you saw me, you looked as if you'd been caught with your hand in the cash register. Why, George?'

She shrugged, her fingers creating a discordant sound. Why couldn't he leave it? Why did he always have to probe at her, seek the reasons for her behaviour? She found words to silence him. 'I thought you might mind. It's your guitar, after all. And I didn't ask if——'

'Why are you lying to me, George?'

She gasped. 'I—how did you know I was lying?'

He brushed the back of his hand across her cheek. 'Honey, your face is so expressive. It's always fascinated me, ever since I saw you last year. When I came in and you saw me, you were back with Scott, weren't you?'

Scott had never wanted her to play the guitar. Why had that been so hard for her to take? It wasn't as if she were a great talent. She didn't need to make music. Her hands fell awkwardly away from the guitar, as if she had forgotten how to play it.

'Only this memory wasn't a happy one?' She shook her head in protest, but Lyle persisted. 'You looked guilty as hell, caught out doing something you shouldn't. Did Scott object to your music?'

She glared at him, said resignedly, 'Damn you, Lyle! It's something to do with your eyes, I think. The rest of you looks like a tough outdoors man, but you've got dreamer's eyes. And you always see too much.'

He lowered himself to sit down beside her. The soft chair shifted to accommodate his weight. His thigh pressed against hers. Somehow the contact seemed comforting, not threatening. 'Why didn't Scott like your playing?'

'Can't you leave it alone?' she asked tiredly.

'No, George, I can't.' He took the hand that rested on the strings, his fingers uncurling hers, as if to make them relax. 'Why didn't he like it?'

'I don't know.' She'd never known, but she had tried. 'I'm such a wild thing. I've always been impulsive, but I tried not to be that way around him. I loved him so much, and I didn't want to spoil it. The music—that was part of it, somehow, because whenever I played I would see that look in his eyes. As if he didn't know what I'd do next.'

He pushed back the hair tumbling over her forehead and she had to look at him. What had Scott wanted of her? Something she couldn't give? Her hair bounced, rubbing across his hand as she shook her head.

'He wanted me to be more grown up, more settled. He was older than me, and I was so young.'

The curls twisted around Lyle's fingers as he mused, 'Volatile, and restless, and full of bouncing enthusiasm.'

Yes, all the wrong things. Scott had wanted her different—stable and content, full of warm acceptance. She said defensively, 'I loved Scott!'

'Past tense?' he asked softly. 'But did Scott love all of you?'

She sagged back against the chair, the guitar slack in her arms. She'd always known that Scott's love depended on her being what he wanted. 'I used to think I could make myself different for him, that I could be like—oh, like Jenny, I guess! Jenny's always known how to please the people she loves, and she doesn't get restless—well, not often, anyway.'

She said tremulously, 'I did love him, and I've missed him terribly, but——'

His hands were gentle through her hair, making her scalp tingle. She blinked against sudden tears that welled up behind her eyes. She thought of all the times she'd turned away from her impulses, of how she'd worried and ached with knowing she couldn't be the perfect wife he wanted. 'I'm never going to do it again. I'm wild and apt to—apt to do any crazy thing. I'm thirty years old now and I'm not going to change.'

His deep eyes held hers with magnetic intensity. 'Grow up, George,' he whispered softly.

'Lyle, I'm thirty years old!'

'Are you?' He was smiling as if at a child. 'Then don't you think it's time you stopped trying to live up to other people's expectations?' His lips brushed hers in the most fleeting of kisses. 'You're one of a kind, sweetheart. Don't let anybody make you feel inadequate for having your own special talents. You don't have to fit into a mould.'

She took a deep breath, tried to conceal that she was trembling from his touch.

He leaned closer, his thigh hard against her as he worked his way around the guitar. His lips moved against her cheek and his low voice said, 'This is my room and it's filled with music. If Scott resented your love of music, I'd say that this is one place you'll have a hard time mixing us up.'

He was right. Here Lyle was strong and alive. His lips found hers. Her hands clenched on the guitar. Her mouth opened as his tongue moved between her lips. When she swayed, he took her closer in his arms and the kiss grew deeper.

His fingers kneaded softly on the muscles of her back, feeling the contours of her spine. When her hands reached up into his hair, her fingers clenched on the slippery softness, pulling him closer as her mouth invited the hard invasion.

His hands on her back, his tongue thrusting, taking possession. A deep shudder passed through the core of her being and her body came to life, shifting closer, seeking intimacy.

The hard edges of the guitar pushed between them in a sudden, painful thrust.

'You're driving me insane,' Lyle groaned as he released her. 'I keep remembering you in my arms, touching you, seeing you in the moonlight.' His breathing was shallow and quick, his eyes flashing as he took in the signs of her own arousal, the thrust of her hardened nipples against her sweater, the rapid rise and fall of her breasts as she tried to calm her breathing. 'You feel the same, don't you? Say it, George!'

The heat was rushing through her body. She gripped the guitar, made music with her fingers that was wilder, more passionate than before.

His voice penetrated the notes. 'George, I want to make love to you.'

'And you want me to stay here?' The words were drawn from her against her will.

'With me,' he said. 'Yes.'

'I can't.' The music came louder. She bent her head over the guitar, said softly, 'It's a trap. Just a little island and the winter storms shutting you in. I could never stay here.'

She pushed the guitar aside and she was on her feet, moving away to stop herself from touching him. She fingered keys on the synthesiser without knowing what they were. 'Can you show me how this thing works?'

'Why not?' He moved close to her and she tensed. He leaned over to turn the power switch on. Over a faint hum, he asked, 'Why did you come sailing up this coast so early in the year?'

She shrugged, moving back a step, out of his reach. 'It's not winter any more. I thought your bad storms were in December and January.'

'The worst ones,' he agreed harshly, 'but March isn't exactly summer. Why didn't you wait for spring? Where were you last? Before you came here?'

She said, 'Mexico,' her voice flat. What was he, psychic? How did he always know where to find her vulnerable spots?

'Mexico?' he repeated, ignoring her unwillingness to talk. 'With the boat? Why did you leave the sunshine? Why not wait until June like the other boats, then come see the North Coast when the sun makes it kind and beautiful?'

'Why do you have to ask so damned many questions?'

He grinned, his long arm reaching her shoulder in a fleeting caress. 'Mostly because you seem to hate answering them so much. That makes you a mystery, honey, and mysteries are for solving.'

'I don't want to be solved.'

Damn! She sounded petulant, like a sulky child. 'I don't want to talk about Mexico,' she added.

'Why not?' He pressed some buttons. The muted sounds of the song he had been writing the night before filled the room. 'So many things you won't talk about. Scott. Your marriage. Mexico—lord! You'd think Mexico would be a safe enough subject. Tell me about the markets, the warm water. Did you swim there? Are sharks a problem for swimmers in Mexico?'

She laughed, then frowned because she didn't want to be smiling at him. She swung away abruptly, stuffing her hands into the pockets of the jeans that were beginning to hurt as they rubbed against the cut on her leg.

'Watch your leg!' His warning came just as she twisted her leg, swinging around at the boundary of the room. She winced at the sudden shaft of pain reaching up her thigh. Then her ribs, seeming belatedly to sense the twisting she had inflicted, hit her with a gaspingly intense attack.

'Are you OK, honey?'

She winced as his hands settled gently over her shoulders. 'Don't touch!' she gasped. 'Please don't touch me for a minute!'

She breathed carefully, slowly making each intake of air longer than the last. 'My poor ribs!'

'Let me see what you've done.' He was frowning, his eyes raking over her. 'You look terribly pale. You're not going to faint, are you?'

'Of course not! I—no, leave it, please!' she protested as his fingers started to pull her sweater up. She wanted so badly to close her eyes, let him take the sweater away. She wanted to give herself to him.

For ever.

No! Not for ever.

'It's all right. Please——'

His fingers stilled, his eyes narrowed as he watched her face. 'OK, be still, George. Come here and sit down for a minute.' He guided her back into the chair. 'Don't try to get up. Just sit down, damn it! Do you ever just sit still and do what you're told?'

She giggled at the frustration in his voice, but let his hands push her back into the chair. Then the pain came and she closed her eyes, whispering. 'No, I guess I don't. When I had chicken-pox as a kid I kept getting out of the house, spreading the pox over the whole neighbourhood.'

'I can believe it.' He prodded gently along her ribcage. 'Stay still for a minute, please, honey. You look terribly pale. I don't think you did any damage, but please try to remember for a while that you're fragile. And I promise I won't ask about Mexico. Now stay still.'

He sat beside her and settled her against his shoulder. 'OK?' he asked, his voice a deep rumble through his chest where her ear pressed against him.

'Yes,' she admitted, giving herself up to the pleasure of resting against him. She seemed to fit so nicely against his shoulder.

His music was low around them, still playing from the recorder connected to his synthesiser. She could hear the water in his music, clear and pale green.

'Mexico wasn't anything really,' she said as his music faded. 'Just—well, depressing, I guess. And I don't feel very good about Mexico. I guess—well, I don't really want you to think badly of me.'

His arms tightened carefully around her. She didn't want to tell him that it hurt when his wrist pushed into her side. She wanted to stay here. In his arms she felt somehow that it was safe to rest, to stop running.

He murmured, 'I don't think I could ever think badly of you.'

It was too easy talking to him. The words just seemed to come of their own volition.

'It started last year. I told you about my cousin Jenny? And Jake? When they finally worked it out, I left them the boat for a honeymoon trip.'

She'd looked down at them from the window of the seaplane as she flew away from them. Together, locked in each other's arms. She'd tried not to envy them their happiness.

Lyle's hand stroked the curls at the back of her neck. 'And what did you do?'

'I went to Montreal for a while. Then I came back and picked up the boat, sailed south. I took my time. It was pretty nice. I was getting into the idea of me-andering around and—I guess it sounds pretty purposeless, doesn't it?'

She'd felt that then, the loneliness growing again, even with the boat running wildly before the wind.

She felt him shrug. The skin of her neck quivered as his thumb brushed the short hairs. 'It depends how you felt about it. It sounds as if you had no worries about money.'

'No.' Her hand was imprisoned between their chests. Her fingers occupied themselves fiddling with the second button on his shirt. 'Scott had a lot of life insurance. He didn't leave it to me as a lump sum. I guess he didn't trust me not to blow it all. So I get an annuity, a monthly cheque from the insurance company. I'd be better off if I had to work, I think, because as it is——'

For the first time it occurred to her that Scott kept her dependent that way, that even now he controlled her life. The thought disturbed her.

'Well, I sailed south, ended up in the Caribbean, anchored at St Thomas in Grenada. Blue seas. Sunshine. Jenny's parents were there. Uncle Herb was teaching at the Technical Institute. They'd just had a letter from Jenny—God, Lyle! I must sound like a sour old maid!'

He chuckled, his lips pressing against the hair at her temple. 'I know the feeling. My family is filled with people who are in love, happily married. Even Con, damn him, seems to be in love with that witch he married. My own marriage was a disaster. I certainly wouldn't wish that on anyone else, but I know how lonely you can feel looking at love from the outside.'

She sighed. She hadn't wanted to be jealous of their love. 'Jenny was expecting a baby and ... I sent them both flowers and got back on *Lady Harriet*. I sailed to Mexico.

'I thought I could spend the winter there. There was— there was a man in a villa nearby.' She shrugged, ignoring the twinge of pain from her ribs. Had she really thought she could heal Scott's desertion with a shallow affair?

She said dully, 'It didn't work. I mean, I tried. I felt so lonely, but——' She didn't look at Lyle. She stared at the button her fingers were twisting, felt the deep, steady motion of his breathing. 'I didn't even say goodbye. I didn't know what to say, and I felt—well, ashamed of myself. He was a nice man and—I pulled the anchor and headed north.

'Once I got going, I couldn't stop. I stopped in Vancouver to see Jenny, but that was all.'

Lyle said softly, 'So you just kept going until you hit Grey Islet?'

She nodded. She'd been running. The weather hadn't mattered. Nothing had mattered.

'And on Wednesday, when you get on that helicopter, where will you go?'

What did it matter where she went? Everywhere was the same. Except here. This island—this man—was something she had to get away from.

'More wandering?' he asked. 'Hop on a plane and visit Paris? Montreal?'

'Vancouver,' she said tonelessly. 'Maybe—I guess I'll buy another guitar. My guitar was on *Lady Harriet*. I'll go to some coffee houses. Get into some jam sessions.'

She thought of trying to drown her memories in music in the city; of Lyle back here on Green Island. Impulsively, she said, 'Lyle, why are you here?'

'It's the best place for Robin right now.' He was shifting, moving away from her. He adjusted something on the synthesiser and she felt cold, sitting alone on the chair. Her ribs had stopped hurting. There was only a dull ache left.

'You can't stay here for ever,' she persisted, not understanding the meaning of the stillness on his face. 'You can't keep hiding yourself and Robin away. Some day you've got to go outside, stop trying to protect her from the hurts and risks of the world.'

She realised suddenly that he was coldly angry. He'd seemed so even tempered, so patient with her, she hadn't known her words could stir him to anger.

He said tightly, 'At least, staying here, Robin and I aren't like you.' He made a sharp gesture towards her small frame in the chair. 'What are you getting from being out in the world you make so much of? What have you got? At least Robin and I have love, and each other.'

George gasped as if he had struck her. She turned away, unable to say anything, a knot of tears gripping her throat.

She scrambled to her feet, moving quickly towards the door. She must escape, get outside quickly before he saw how much his words had hurt.

'George——' He reached out to hold her back and she jerked away, her face averted.

'Let me go, Lyle! Let me out of here!'

Then she was running, through the door, outside and down the boardwalk in her bare feet, ignoring the cramping spasms from her leg.

She would always be alone. There'd never be another Scott, because she couldn't bring herself to trust like that again. There were no children. No one.

Jenny. She could hold Jenny's baby, be an aunt.

It wasn't enough!

She left the boardwalk, her bare feet cold on the wet grass. She came to a stop at the edge of the lawn, looking out over the water.

She could hear him following, feel his presence as he came up behind her. She said bitterly, 'Is there nowhere to get away from you? I can't run away from you, can't go anywhere. This damned island is too bloody small!'

'George, I'm sorry.' His hands cupped her shoulders and pulled her back against his muscular chest. 'I don't know why I said a thing like that, but—I guess you must have gotten me where it hurt. I hit back without thinking. I'm sorry.'

She wished she could cry. He was holding her and she wanted badly to put her face against his shoulder and let the tears come.

'I'm sorry too,' she said wearily. 'I didn't mean to hurt you or—you seemed so impervious, so sure of what you were doing here.' She smiled, turning to look at him. 'How was I to know you had any tender spots?'

His arms tightened, then dropped as he saw her face in the sweep of the lighthouse beam. 'Sorry, that's hurting your ribs, isn't it? You look so—it's hard to keep remembering you were so badly beaten up only a few days ago. Come back and sing for me. We won't argue any more now.'

She laughed, letting him take her arm and turn her towards the house. 'Won't we? I wouldn't count on that.' The way the feelings seemed to boil up in her when he was near, she doubted if they could ever go long without some kind of argument.

'I've been out here five years with Robin.' He was looking down at her, his head a dark silhouette against the sky. 'When Hazel left me, Robin seemed terrified that I would leave, too. She clung to me, cried whenever I went away.'

George touched the fingers of her free hand to his lips. 'Lyle, you don't need to explain to me.'

'I was flying helicopters. I was away a lot—sometimes a charter would take me away for two or three days, sometimes longer. I had to make a living to support Robin. My mother wanted me to send her down to stay with them, but she seemed to need me—yet my job was impossible for a single parent. I thought of the light-houses. It seemed ideal. I could make a living, keep Robin with me all the time.'

George took his hands in her own. His seemed tense and unresponsive until he closed them on hers. She wanted to ease his distress. 'Robin's getting older,' she said hesitantly. 'Don't you think——'

'Yes,' he agreed. 'But I've got to figure out a way to manage it. I haven't made my fortune writing songs yet, and any flying job would be impossible still. I can't be an absentee father to Robin. She needs more than that.'

'Robin's a lucky girl,' she said, looking around at the island, back to the man who was her father. She pulled on his hands. 'Let's go in and do your song.'

His eyes focused on her, a smile in them. 'I've always wanted to find someone with a good voice to record with. I record my own voice because it's all I've got to show the words, but I'm no singer.'

'Lyle, I'm not—you're not planning to record me?'

But he was, and she found that she didn't really mind. She'd performed for small audiences before, but singing for Lyle had its own special magic. Lyle, watching, his fingers bringing the music up to meet her voice, down to soft silence. Then, afterwards, playing it back, their music filling the small sound-proofed room.

'It's amazing!' breathed George. 'My voice isn't really that powerful. You must have done magic with those dials and buttons you've got. It really sounds professional.'

'Close,' Lyle agreed. 'I'd like to take it and get it mixed down in a studio—I've got a friend in Victoria who could do it for us.'

'Us? You mean you want to try to sell this tape? My voice singing your song?'

'Why not?'

Scott's disapproval was the only reason why not.

Lyle inserted another tape into the recorder. 'If you stayed for a while, we could do more—enough for an album.'

She stood up abruptly. This was a magic room. Lyle and the music. Lyle's eyes on her, deep and blue.

He said, 'I'd get it mixed down, send it to my talent agent. Together, I bet we could make something of it.'

She strummed the guitar softly. It sounded like a fantasy, a dream. Making music with him, playing and singing. In this room, the music seemed to draw them together, to a closeness beyond anything physical. Inside these four walls there was only strength and closeness and—love.

'If I stayed, singing isn't the only thing that would happen.'

He said softly, 'That's for damned sure!' and she laughed, although her heart was pounding hard and she wanted to step closer to him. If she set the guitar aside and crossed the room to him, they would be lovers. Would his strong hands tremble as they took the barrier of clothes from between them?

'It's time I went to bed,' she whispered, then felt heat flooding over her face as his eyes flared; but 'Goodnight,' was all he said. She could feel his eyes on her back as she walked through the door. Upstairs, she spent a long moment standing over Robin's bed, looking down on the sleeping child. Below her, a door closed. Lyle going outside.

It was a long night, and she didn't sleep well.

The next day Robin spent the morning over at Russ's house, where her uncle was supervising her mathematics test. Lyle was working on the malfunctioning generator again. George watched him for a while, but he didn't seem to want or need help, so she went back to the house, looking for something to do.

She felt the wild restlessness building. She was afraid that if she didn't keep herself busy, she might do something crazy.

Later, when she took coffee out to Lyle, he was elbow-deep in oil and generator parts. He looked at his black hands, then the cup.

'The cup will wash,' she said, laughing.

He took a big mouthful of the coffee. Then he set it down and she thought he would probably forget it was there. His eyes were on the mess of parts in front of him.

She couldn't help feeling that he'd always been just outside the door, or just in the next room. Even the grease on his hands seemed familiar.

She looked at the engine, said, 'I thought you were going to send for a repairman for that?'

'Well——' he shrugged self-consciously '—it's not really my job, messing around with these generators, but I think I can get it going again.'

'You're having fun,' she accused. 'You enjoy being up to your elbows in grease.'

His eyes took on a mischievous light. 'Right now, I'd enjoy kissing you. With that oversized shirt blowing around you, and your hair tumbled all around your face, I——'

She felt her body responding to his words, said hurriedly, 'There's grey in that hair. I'm far too old for being grabbed by boys with black grease on their hands.'

'Wanna bet?' he threatened softly, coming to his feet and stepping closer to her, his hands at his sides. 'I'd say there's a lot of fire in the old lady yet.'

She caught his eyes and found herself laughing. 'No, I'm not rising to your bait, you devious man! Go back to your engine——'

'Generator,' he corrected mildly.

'Generator, then. If you're good, you can come for lunch in about an hour. The pizza should be done about then.'

'Pizza?' He shook his head regretfully, his hands busy already with a wrench and a black-coated piece of metal. 'It sounds lovely, but there's no pizza in the freezer.'

'You don't get pizza from the freezer, you innocent! You make bread and take some of the dough off for pizza. You roll it out thin and spread on tomato sauce. Slice on some mushrooms and pepperoni and shavings of cheese and——'

'Stop!' he begged. 'You're torturing me. When you talk like that, my stomach thinks it didn't have breakfast. I thought you said you weren't much of a cook? You told me you were a woman of the world—walk into a restaurant and order your food. Can you really bake bread?'

'One of my few culinary talents. Do a good job on that engine—generator—and I might reward you. But only if you wash before you come to the table.'

She went back into the house, feeling warm and content, happier than she could remember feeling in years.

She wished he'd taken her in his arms and kissed her, grease or not.

CHAPTER SEVEN

IN THE afternoon, looking out through the window while Robin worked at the table, George saw Lyle talking to Russ, standing with his thumbs hooked loosely in his belt, his hair glinting in the sunlight. She almost went down to him, to catch at his hand and feel him close.

The day after tomorrow she'd be gone. She tried to imagine Montreal, or even Paris. She felt she should go somewhere French, but she wished she could feel more excited about going.

Before she left, she could go to him.

At night, if she slipped into his room——

Tonight he would ask her down to his music-room. They would work together. She'd ask to sing some of his other songs. Then, when they were sharing that special intimacy that music brought, she would——

How did a woman go about asking a man? She'd never learned to be assertive about physical intimacies. Scott had wanted her soft and accepting. He'd always been the one to do the asking. For the first time, it occurred to her that the physical side of their life together had been geared to his needs, not hers. Surely she wouldn't actually have to *ask* Lyle? He'd admitted he wanted her. And tonight, if she waited, if she didn't run away when he came close...

She got all the laundry done and hung out on the clothes-line, thankful that Lyle didn't seem to notice what she was doing. She didn't want to have to defend her unaccustomed domestic urges. After lunch she started ironing Lyle's shirts, ignoring Robin's protest that her dad never ironed them unless he was going to town.

She and Robin worked to make a newspaper pattern from Robin's favourite skirt, then Robin pulled out the Sears catalogue and they picked fabrics the girl could order to make the new skirt. George realised she should never have started this project. She would be gone when the fabric came, and Robin hardly knew how to use the sewing machine that was stored away in a cupboard.

'Maybe your Aunt Dorothy could help you,' George said slowly.

Robin nodded, frowning. 'I guess,' she said flatly, closing the catalogue with a slap, and coming unsteadily to her feet.

Lyle brought Russ for dinner. The younger man prowled the kitchen, restless and worried.

He kept saying, 'I can hardly wait to see Dorothy.'

George managed to stop his pacing by handing him a bottle of beer and waving him into a chair, although her mind was on Lyle, wondering why he'd greeted her so abruptly. Had she done something to make him angry? 'How long have you been married?' she asked Russ.

'Just a year.' Russ had been yearning for a chance to talk about Dorothy. He'd met her at a going-away party for a friend who was emigrating to Australia. She was a year older than him, and beautiful—at least, he thought so.

'She *is* beautiful,' George agreed. 'I've seen your wedding picture. Robin showed me.'

He cupped his hands around the beer bottle. 'The night I met her, I told her I wished I'd stayed at university.' He laughed. 'The next thing I knew I was married to her, and applying for a job as a lightkeeper so I could support us while I finished my degree through the Open Learning Institute.' He chuckled again, grinning as he admitted, 'She's got me wrapped around her little finger. I do whatever she tells me.'

Russ kept talking all through dinner. His conversation covered Lyle's silence.

Robin, at first silently glum, cheered up as they ate.

'When you've got the baby I could baby-sit,' she offered shyly.

'You sure could!' Russ agreed.

Encouraged, she asked suddenly, 'Could I come see the baby being born?' Russ choked on his beer.

Lyle stayed silent through it all. George kept glancing at him, then looking away quickly because his eyes weren't on her and she didn't want to be caught staring as if she were a young girl with a painful crush. He seemed to come to life as George got up to clear the table. 'Sit back down, George. I'll do that.'

She shook her head, but she let him help her stack the dishes. Russ and Robin moved into the living-room with the dog. George's eyes followed them as she started to wash the dishes. 'I think Russ and Dorothy are lucky,' she said softly to Lyle.

He carefully polished the glass she had just washed. 'How long were you and Scott married?'

For once, she didn't mind talking about Scott. He's gone, she thought, and it didn't hurt. Even his memory seemed to be losing its sharpness.

'Nine years. Almost ten.' She moved a stack of plates into the dishwater. 'What about you and Hazel?'

'Four,' he said abruptly. 'Why didn't you have any children? You wanted them.'

How did he know that? She stared down into the dishwater, remembering the arguments. Only two things they'd argued about. Her music. Her wanting children.

She said slowly, her eyes riveted to the water, 'He didn't think it was a good idea. I kept trying to change his mind, but...'

Lyle took another glass from the draining-board. He was losing ground with the drying, the dishes stacking up on the draining-board. 'Perhaps it's just as well you didn't succeed. It's dangerous to push people into parenting when they're not ready.'

Maybe that was true. She'd wanted children, but she wouldn't have wanted to make Scott an unwilling father.

Scott had had faults, just as she had. Somehow, she'd never acknowledged that before.

Lyle's hair was falling across his forehead again, although now it was short enough that it couldn't reach his eyes. She wanted to brush it back with her fingers.

He said, 'Hazel didn't want children. I thought she'd feel differently about it once it happened, and I was stupid enough to think it would be all right if there was a child. I tricked her—I told her there wouldn't be a child, that I would look after it.'

His eyes followed hers into the next room, where Robin was brushing the dog while she talked to her uncle eagerly. 'Of course, I'm glad to have Robin, but it was wrong of me.'

She scrubbed carefully at a stubborn spot on one of the plates. She didn't know what to say, but she wanted to give him something, to tell him he should stop feeling guilty.

'I used to sneak out on Scott,' she said in a low voice, giving him her confession because she had nothing else to give. 'He hated me to go to the coffee houses, hated me singing and playing in public. When he was out, I'd take my guitar out of the closet and go downtown. I always felt so guilty about it. Once he came and found me. I felt like a naughty child.' She stared at the plate that was long since scrubbed clean. 'I loved him, but he treated me like a child.'

In the beginning it had been a dream come true. 'It was years before I started resenting the way he controlled my life. In the beginning, I was so busy clinging to him, I'd have tried to be anything he wanted.'

Lyle took her left hand in his, lifting it wet and dripping from the water. He said gently, 'You loved him, and I'm sure he loved you. Even good marriages have their ups and downs. Eventually you'd have asserted yourself. If he loved you, he'd have accepted it.'

Having Scott as the masterful husband had made her feel secure, had comforted the child who'd lost her father. When Scott died, the child had been in the process of growing up, of rebelling against his authority. And, like a child, she'd felt guilty about the rebellion, felt that she'd betrayed him by trying to be herself.

Was that right? Somehow she'd been feeling guilty, as if she were in the wrong, as if she'd never be able to live up to anyone's expectations of her.

What if that was wrong? What if——

She drew back from the idea.

'Are you going to wear that ring for ever?' Lyle asked, his fingers on her wedding ring.

Until death do us part ... It was a barrier between her and Lyle. She pulled away. 'I don't know.'

His hand clenched on hers. 'Don't go, darling. You're like the sun—alive and vibrant, bringing warmth and light. Stay here, George. Let that helicopter go without you.'

She thrust her hands back into the water, wincing as she splashed water on to her face. She said slowly, 'Lyle, you want me to stay, but I'm not a person who's good at staying. I—I do silly things.'

Was it so bad to be impulsive and emotional? Scott hadn't liked it, but—— Tonight was no night for starting an affair. Lyle had come too close. Anything started now might turn into more than she could handle. 'I need time,' she said desperately.

'Take all the time you need.' His hand still held hers as he said, 'You know where to find me,' then he released her.

They played canasta after the dishes were done. Robin was obviously accustomed to playing cards with the adults. She was a sharp player, with surprisingly good concentration. Russ was her partner, but they lost badly because he didn't have his mind on the game.

George was relieved to be playing cards. If she and Lyle had gone down to the music-room, she was afraid he'd have sensed her earlier intention to start an affair with him. This island must be getting to her brain! What kind of insanity was it to think of intimacy with this man? He needed far more of a woman than she could give. He needed a wife and a mother for his daughter, and George was the last person to supply those needs. All her life people had been telling her she was irresponsible and immature. Lyle had had one irresponsible wife. He surely didn't need another.

And she didn't need another husband. It was time she grew up and learned to be happy without needing a man to lean on.

That sounded hollow, an empty fate.

When Robin started yawning, George pushed her cards to one side and said, 'Kiss the men goodnight, Robin, and I'll tuck you in. I'm ready for bed myself.'

She watched Robin giving both Lyle and Russ an affectionate kiss, and an extra hearty hug for her father. She avoided meeting Lyle's eyes as he looked up from his daughter, but her heart was pounding as she took Robin's hand.

'Goodnight, Russ. Lyle.'

Russ nodded. Lyle said, 'Have a good sleep,' softly, as if he knew that she would be lying awake.

'I will,' she agreed brightly, walking away from him. She could feel his eyes on her. She clenched Robin's hand tighter, feeling as if she were walking from the warm into the cold snow. She read a story for Robin, then let herself be talked into reading another.

In bed, alone, she tried to imagine what her life would be like today if Scott were alive. She couldn't bring his features to life in her mind.

She would have been a different woman, less independent, softer. She'd just spent three years alone, and the image of the woman Scott's wife would have been seemed far from reality. As Scott was far from reality. Loved, but gone away. She wasn't the same woman who had loved Scott.

She shivered, cold under the warm blankets. If Scott had lived, they both might have changed, but he'd died. And she had changed. And today, now, she didn't want to be Scott Dobson's wife.

Morning came. She found the kitchen empty, a pound of bacon open on the counter, the frying-pan warming on the stove. Lyle and Robin must be close by. George started cooking the bacon. When Lyle came, she was thankful that he was alone. She didn't want to mention leaving when Robin was present.

'Have a good sleep?' He was half smiling, seeing her face still flushed with sleep.

'Yes.' She hadn't expected to sleep well, but she had. 'Lyle, if I'm leaving tomorrow——'

'If?'

His eyes narrowed and she said quickly, 'I mean, when I go—I forgot about it, but what you said before——' She sounded like a foundering teenager. She took a deep breath, and tried to sound as if she had control of her mind and her tongue. 'I don't have any money, and no identification. I should have called Jenny, but it's too late now. Can I—do you have any money you would lend me?'

He took her place at the stove. 'I'll look after that. It's one of my few culinary talents, making bacon. I've got a bit of cash, not a lot. You're welcome to what I've got. There's not much need for money out here, and in Prince Rupert I write cheques mostly. But don't worry about it. I'll give you my credit card. You should be able to do pretty well anything with that—hotels, restaurants.'

'I can't use your credit card!' You used a husband's credit card, not a friend's. Not even—a lover's. Using his card seemed like a commitment, a statement that they had a relationship. That she was dependent on him.

He shrugged. 'You don't have much choice, if you want to go into town. Where's your bank? Vancouver? Victoria? Use my card until you get there, then you'll be able to get your identification straightened out, get a new cheque book and so forth. You can pay me back and send the card back by registered mail.'

She glared at him. 'Lyle, you can't give your credit card to a total stranger! Only an idiot would do something like that. Why, I could do anything with that card!'

He wanted to tell her that he didn't care, that she could spend his whole credit limit and it would be more than worth it, just to have had her near for a few days. He wanted to tell her that giving her the card might make a tie that would bring her back. Perhaps she'd come and return it in person.

He couldn't say any of it. He wanted to reach out to her, take her in his arms. Last night he had almost asked her down to his music-room again, knowing that her presence there might well end with them sharing a bed. Every time he looked at her, thought of her, he ached with wanting her. More than once he'd seen indications that she shared at least some of his need. He thought that he could seduce her if he tried. He was terrified that he would lose control of himself and his sanity, and actually find himself using their sexual attraction as a lever to try to make her stay with him.

Hadn't he learned his lesson from Hazel? He wanted George, needed her with a desperation that shocked him, but he dared not exert pressure on her. A gift of love was worthless unless it was freely given.

It was the smell of burning bacon that brought him back to the kitchen, to George staring at him. He

couldn't help smiling at her anger at his apparent care-
lessness with his credit card.

'You're no stranger,' he said mildly, reconstructing
their conversation, turning the bacon. 'I'd trust you with
a lot more than my credit cards. Are you going to
Vancouver first?'

'Yes, I'll go to Jenny for a few days while I get
organised.'

What then? What would she do next? She had to have
a plan, a goal. If she wasn't going somewhere, doing
something——

Maybe it was time for that. Time to stop and face
everything, stop running from herself.

'Would you do me a favour? While you've got my
card, could you go shopping for a present for Robin for
me? Her birthday's coming up at the beginning of May
and I honestly don't know what she wants! You've been
spending a lot of time with her. If you could think of
something she'd like, I'd appreciate it if you could pick
it up and mail it to me here. Would you mind?'

Her face cleared. She'd go shopping as soon as she
got to Vancouver. She'd enjoy that, buying a gift for
Robin. 'Of course I don't mind!'

He hoped she'd never learn that he had Robin's present
already bought and paid for, safely hidden in a cupboard
in Russ's house. Meanwhile, he was glad to have found
a way she could accept the use of his credit card without
any further protest.

He wanted to spend the rest of the day with her, but
he didn't trust himself not to put pressure on her to stay.
She wasn't ready to stay. Perhaps she never would be,
but she had said that she needed time, and he was determined to give her whatever time she needed, to hope
that she would come back one day.

He had to fight his frightened conviction that she
would walk away and he would never see her again. He
did it by spending the day with a series of tasks that

could easily have been put off until tomorrow, or even next month. He tested the drinking water in the cisterns, went up the light tower to check that the change-over relay was working, and to clean and polish the tower windows.

When he looked down from the tower and saw George and Robin walking slowly over the beach, he resisted the impulse to go down to be with them.

When the day was over, he encouraged Russ to stay for a game of cards again, playing until Robin was yawning and George took her off to bed.

For a while he even had himself believing that when she left, he would stop wanting her. Then, the instant she walked down the hallway, he was afraid that she wouldn't come back, that he wouldn't get a chance to say goodnight to her properly, that the chopper would come early the next day and she'd leave without his having any chance to say any of the things burning inside him.

Russ asked, 'Why don't you ask her to stay?'

'Why don't you mind your own business?' Lyle said harshly, then immediately wished the words unsaid because Russ was pushing to his feet, angry and sulky.

'I don't need telling twice,' his kid brother muttered, pushing the chair in to the table, slamming out of the kitchen door.

Damn! Lyle started after him, hesitated, then shrugged. What could he say? It wouldn't help anything to rush after his baby brother to talk about his love for a woman he'd known only days. Maybe Russ would understand. After all, he said he'd loved Dorothy the instant he saw her across that smoke-filled room.

Love.

He listened to George's door close, strained his ears for the sounds of her getting ready for bed. Might she come back out? Could he go down the hallway, knock softly on her door and ask her to sing for him again tonight?

If he asked, would she come?

If she came downstairs, she would sing his love songs. He could watch her fingers stroking the guitar strings, her eyes dropping as her voice took on a husky seductiveness.

The next song would be for her. She was filled with the contradictions the best songs were made of. His stray lady. Wild lady, with love spilling over for everyone she came near. Stray lady, afraid to love again.

Stray lady, let me love you.

He went outside, walking the island in the dark, the notes of his love song for George ringing in his mind. When he came back, the house was dark. He looked in on Robin. She was sleeping with her lips parted and the Walkman headphones on her ears. He took the headphones off and covered her. She'd be nine in a few weeks. Did other nine-year-old girls live with their stereos plastered to their ears?

George said he should get off this island, take Robin back into the city. He shivered, remembering the last weeks of their time in town, Robin's withdrawal from everyone but him, her certainty that everyone was watching her, revolted by the accident of birth that had crippled her leg. Perhaps it *was* time to go back, but he was frightened of failing, of seeing Robin hurt.

He went downstairs, to listen to the recording George had made with him. He'd built it up with his multi-track recorder. The drums...then the bass guitar. Layer on layer...then George's husky voice blending with the instruments. It was good. He had to listen hard to pick up the faults that came from recording in an imperfect studio. When he got it mixed down, it would be a superb recording. A winner.

He was afraid the tape might be all he'd ever have of her. He had already made a copy of it, in case something happened to the original. Now he connected the cassette recorder and made another copy, this one for George.

What else could he give her to remember him?

Her recorded voice was fading to an echo in the room when she opened the door and slipped silently inside. She was dressed in the jeans and light T-shirt she'd been wearing under her cruiser suit when he'd pulled her out of the ocean. He remembered the feel of her, wet and unconscious in his arms. She leaned back on the door, her weight pushing it closed. Motionless, silent, she stared at him.

Had his own need brought her? Or was she awake from dreams of another man, another love? She was breathing quickly, her breasts rising and falling, the soft, unrestrained swell revealing that she wasn't wearing her bra. Her nipples were erect, thrust against the fabric. His mouth went dry.

She moved one small step further into the room.

His voice was hoarse as he asked, 'Do you want to sing?' His shaking fingers threw a switch. Drums beat softly in the silent room. A bass guitar strummed. She shook her head silently. Her eyes surveyed the room, taking everything in as if she were seeing it for the first time. He watched her rub her palms down along her thighs and realised that she was at least as nervous as he was.

George. She was an assertive lady, accustomed to speaking her mind, asking for what she wanted. Right now she was frozen, speechless. Shy.

'What do you want, George?' He could hardly talk.

'I——' Her tongue just touched the pink fullness of her lips as he watched. She took a deep breath. Her breasts strained against the shirt, the nipples still rigidly erect.

He found himself standing, pushing himself away from the console. He saw her eyes take in the length of his body, the evidence of his own need as he stood.

He watched the motion of her throat as she swallowed with difficulty. 'Lyle,' she whispered, her eyes finding his, 'please—touch me.'

She hadn't known what she was going to say, had hoped words would not be necessary. As if her voice had released him, he took two long steps towards her. Her breath came short, almost panting as he approached. She was trembling, waiting for his touch, but he lifted only her hand, brushing his lips softly across her knuckles.

'Touch you?' he asked softly, his breath warm on her wrist. 'Like that?'

She wanted more, his arms around her, taking her close. She wanted to close her eyes and give herself up to his touch.

'Is this what you want?' he asked again, some instinct urging him to hold back. He turned her hand, pressed his lips against her sensitive palm, traced the lines of her hand with his damp tongue.

'Lyle,' she whispered, shuddering.

He had both her hands in his, his hands gripping hers to stop his own trembling. He was pressing soft kisses against her palms, licking gently at the inner sides of her wrists, making her tremble with a terrible need that surged like fire through her veins.

His lips traced up the inner surface of her forearm to her elbow. Her blood was turning to flames. A groan escaped her lips, a wordless plea for his lips hard against hers, his arms holding her.

'What are you doing?' she asked desperately, as he pulled back. He kept hold of her hands, but he was a foot away, his eyes touching the swelling of her breasts. How could he step back when she felt this terrible, wild need? Her tongue touched her lips and found them swollen, as if he had been kissing her.

His eyes held hers. She couldn't conceal her arousal. She felt nervous, vulnerable, but she wanted him to see

her need. He let go her left hand and slowly, softly
brushed the palm of his hand over the thrusting nipple
of her right breast. She gasped and bit her lip to stop
from groaning aloud.

His voice was a harsh whisper as he said, 'I'm trying
to make you want me, George.' Both his hands covered
the swelling of her breasts in a fleeting erotic caress. 'I
want to make sure you know whose arms are holding
you.'

She shivered at his reminder of the heated dream she'd
woken from only days ago.

'Lyle, I——' Her words were lost as his lips touched
hers. He brushed a gentle kiss on her lips, then traced
the fullness of her parted lips with his tongue. Her lips
parted farther, inviting him to deepen the kiss. Instead,
he drew back.

She shivered, standing alone. 'Lyle, what do you want
of me?' She could hardly breathe. She needed his touch,
his hard arms, his hands on her naked flesh. 'It's you,'
she whispered. 'I can't sleep for dreaming about you.
I—— Please, I'm not good at this. I've never—I don't
know how to do this,' she admitted helplessly.

'Then kiss me,' he ordered roughly. 'Don't talk.'

She reached her hands up, threaded fingers through
his waving hair and pulled his mouth down to hers. Then
his arms slid around her back and pulled her close as
his lips took hers...softly, then harder, drawing her
shyness away. Her hands were moving, feeling out the
contours of his heavily muscled shoulders, her lips open
wide to his kiss. She moved, feeling her breasts pushing
hard against his chest.

When she felt him moving away, her need had grown
so great that she didn't hesitate to whisper a plea, 'No,
please! Please, don't stop. Lyle...'

His husky laugh turned into a groan. 'Honey, I'm not.
Come here.' He urged her down on to the thick, soft
carpet, whispering, 'With you touching me, your body

soft against me, I'm shaking so badly I don't think I can stand up a moment longer.'

She trembled, feeling the heat of him as he drew her close in his arms. A hot pulse was beating somewhere near the centre of her. He was leaning back on a cushion, with her cradled against his chest. Her hands fumbled against his shirt, then slipped inside, feeling the roughness of the hairs growing on his chest, spreading out to feel his skin against her palms, her eyelids dropping with passion as she touched him.

He groaned aloud as her fingers glided over his tight, male nipples, then his arms were hard around her, pulling her up over him. His hands slid up under her thin shirt, exploring the shape of her back, his fingers rough and callused on her white skin. When he pushed the shirt up, she found her arms lifting to help him.

Then her swollen breasts felt the roughness of the hair on his chest and she lifted her arms, pulling his head down to her lips again, the tension of her lifted arms pressing her softness against him.

Spinning... music soft in her ears... heated lips on her face, her neck. His lips left her skin, she dragged her eyes open to see his face only inches away, bathed in the soft light from a lamp on the other side of the room.

She saw him watching her mouth, as her tongue wetted her swollen lips, felt some wanton part of her responding to what happened in his eyes as he saw her arousal. When he leaned back from her, his skin pulled against hers and his eyes followed the curve of her throat, the rising swelling of her breasts. She pulled a deep breath in, feeling her chest rise and his own breath catch in his throat as he watched her.

She was amazed at the excitement growing in her, just from watching his eyes watching her, wanting her. She whispered his name and touched his face softly, fleetingly with her fingers.

'Cold?' he asked as her flesh trembled.

'No,' she breathed, her eyes telling him why she trembled.

'George.' His mouth formed the name, his lips coming closer, brushing her throat, then lower to the swelling his eyes had caressed so heatedly. 'I love calling you George,' he said, his lips drawing one rosy peak into his mouth. She writhed in his arms, clutching at his shoulders, thrusting herself against him. His hands dropped to her hips, pulling her close against him as his tongue drew softly over her aching flesh. 'You're so damned feminine,' he whispered, his lips moving to the lobe of her ear. 'All woman...soft and hot and loving...'

She lost track of the words. There was only the heat and the needing...his hands...his lips...her own hands boldly fumbling with the belt buckle at his waist...the rough feel of her jeans being pushed down along the skin of her legs. The shuddering sweet agony of his leg thrust against the hot, naked skin of her thigh.

Then there were no words, only soft sounds of need from her throat and from his. His hands... Oh, God! His hands touching places she had never known were for touching, for loving...and his kisses everywhere...his skin warm and man-rough under her lips and her fingers.

He was driving her beyond sanity with his touch and his breath on her skin. She was wild, writhing in his arms, need exploding through her and giving words to her impassioned moans.

'Please...' Her fingers dug into the knotted muscles at his back. She couldn't open her eyes, but she could feel what would be in his deep blue gaze. 'Now,' she whispered, the restraint that Scott had taught her long forgotten.

She gasped as he shifted over her, trembling, waiting, needing.

There was a terrible stillness, then his hand resting on the trembling flesh at her waist. She felt a shudder run through his body, then he drew back from her.

'George, you—honey, you're not prepared for this, are you?'

'What?' The air seemed abruptly cool. He was staring at her, some pain deep in the blue eyes. She shivered. 'What do you mean?'

His hand moved along her soft skin, settled on the gentle curve of her abdomen. 'You're not on the Pill, or—or anything like that. And, out here—I don't have any way to protect you.'

She closed her eyes briefly, painfully sucking in a deep breath. He pulled her heated flesh closer and she felt him all along the length of her. 'It doesn't matter,' she whispered. She found his hand and brought it against her breast, shuddering as he touched her.

He jerked away, staggering slightly as he got to his feet. He stared down at her and she felt her arms coming up to cover herself from his eyes.

'It matters.' His voice lashed her harshly.

'I'll have your child,' she whispered. 'Give me your child, Lyle.' She felt the fullness in her abdomen, a sudden overwhelming desire for the knowledge of life growing in her.

He moved away from her, jerked his jeans from a tumbled pile of clothing on the floor. His face was hard, but she saw his fingers trembling on the belt. 'Don't talk,' he ordered her harshly. 'You're a passionate woman who's been alone too long. Right now you'd say anything. In the morning you'd be running for that helicopter.'

He laughed harshly. 'I've made one mess already. My daughter has no mother. I'm damned if I'll father a child I might never see.'

She couldn't move, couldn't bring her arms up to cover herself. She couldn't take in his words. Later, their meaning would come to her, hard and painful with the daylight. His eyes were on her and he could see everything. She knew she should be scrambling for her clothes, covering herself, but she still needed his possession of her with a pain that was growing into a hard knot at her centre.

He managed to get the belt of his jeans fastened. He gave her one last harsh stare and walked out of the room, closing the door behind him and leaving her alone on the carpeted floor, staring at the jumble of his shirt mixed up with her own clothes.

CHAPTER EIGHT

'...ANNOUNCES that the arrival of flight 302 from Victoria will be delayed...' The loudspeaker was drowned out by the clatter of dishes from a nearby cafeteria, concluding with '...five-twenty.'

Twenty minutes more.

George ducked around a young couple dragging a screaming toddler, found herself a quiet spot in a bookshop that opened on to the airport waiting-room. She felt the full skirt settling around her legs as she stopped moving. Nearby, a businessman glanced away from the book display on the wall and let his eyes travel appreciatively over her feminine curves.

Lyle had never seen her in a skirt. Would he like it? Would he notice that the blue matched her eyes?

Would he be happy to see her?

He'd been so silent the morning she had left. Robin had cried, throwing herself into George's arms, while Lyle stood rigidly behind his daughter, his hands deep in his pockets, his eyes searching the sky for the helicopter that they could already hear.

The last minutes had passed so quickly. The big machine landed on the pad, the doors were thrown open and a mail bag was thrown out. Russ had pulled her arm and she'd suddenly been half-way up the steps into the chopper, looking back and finding Lyle walking away with the man who had got off the helicopter, moving quickly towards where Robin was sitting in the trailer of the tractor waiting for him. He was carrying the mail bag and he didn't look back.

Look back, she'd pleaded silently, but he hadn't heard. It was as if he wanted her to go. Russ sat beside her,

139

belted her in when her own fingers fumbled, then handed her a small package that lay limp in her hands.

'It's from Lyle,' he'd said curtly, before moving forward to talk to the radio operator.

She fumbled with the flap of the big envelope. Fifty dollars. His credit card. A cassette tape with her name written on the label. A slip of paper with his mailing address written on it, but not another word.

She hadn't let herself cry, but she knew the tears would come the moment she was alone. They'd landed at the coastguard base in Prince Rupert. Someone had called a taxi and Russ had ushered her into the back seat, himself in the front. Before leaving the base, Russ had made a phone call and determined that Dorothy was once again in hospital, this time in labour.

'I'll get you settled in a hotel first,' he'd muttered as they got into the taxi.

'I'm fine,' she'd protested, feeling his disapproval and not knowing just what Lyle might have said to him or what he was thinking of her.

'Lyle said to look after you,' he'd insisted stubbornly.

'I don't need looking after.' She had to be alone. She leaned forward and told the taxi driver, 'The hospital first, please. Then—could you recommend a central hotel? In walking distance to everything?'

'The Rupert Hotel,' the driver said. Russ said, 'The Crest.'

'The Rupert, then,' said George. Russ shrugged and had the sense to let her have her way.

George would have liked to see Dorothy, to see the baby through the nursery windows after it was born. Seeing the baby would have made her feel that she was part of Lyle's family. She wanted to be part of his family. Why was she leaving, when everything inside her was crying for her to stay? This morning, if he had asked her to stay, she thought she might have said yes.

She checked into the hotel. Her room had a window on the ocean. She stared out, seeing the water and wondering what Lyle would be doing now. The relief light-keeper had stepped off the helicopter as she and Russ got on. He and Lyle would probably be talking, going over the temporary man's duties. If she had stayed, they could have done more songs. At night, when Robin went to sleep, she and Lyle could go downstairs and close the door on the world.

She thought about the seaplane companies she knew were based here. She could charter a plane—would they take Lyle's credit card? In a couple of hours she could be back on Green Island. She hadn't realised that walking away from Lyle would hurt so much. She'd told herself that it was a sexual thing, that she could have an affair with him and be free of it. Last night she'd tried to lose herself in his arms. He hadn't let her, had insisted she see the possible consequences of their passion.

Babies. Love. He hadn't said that he loved her, but she had seen it in his eyes. She was almost certain that he did. He wanted her to come back, yet she was afraid of losing herself in his strength, terrified she wouldn't be able to be what he wanted of her. She was almost positive she couldn't live in a place like that, shut off from the world, immobilised on an isolated island.

She loved him.

No!

When had that happened?

It couldn't work. She'd never been able to be what Scott wanted. It would be the same with Lyle. He wanted her to stay with him, to embrace his lighthouse life along with himself and Robin.

She turned away from the window, picked up the telephone.

Jenny's voice came warm over the wire, 'Yes, of course I'll accept the charges. George, are you all right? Where are you calling from?'

'Prince Rupert. And I'm OK.' She closed her eyes and pictured Jenny, surrounded with pieces of video tape, Jake somewhere behind her getting excited over the newest film.

'When the operator said you were calling collect, I thought something must be wrong.' Jenny's laughter came clearly as she asked, 'Surely you didn't forget to pay the bill on your telephone calling-card? Did they cut you off?' It was the sort of thing George might do, forgetting to pay because she was busy getting into an adventure somewhere.

'I lost the card,' George admitted. 'I lost *Lady Harriet*.'

'What?' Jenny squealed. 'What did you say?'

'I sank her. I'm OK, but *Lady Harriet* is wrecked on a rock near Green Island lighthouse.'

George heard Jake's voice in the background, then Jenny asking quietly, 'George, are you sure you're OK?'

'I'm fine. Really, Jenny. I've just got to get my paperwork straightened out. I've lost my wallet and my cheque book.'

'I'll wire you a plane ticket,' her cousin said quickly. 'Prince Rupert? You can pick it up at the travel agent there.'

'No, don't. I don't need it.'

She was going to use Lyle's credit card. She wanted the symbolic intimacy of using his card.

Jenny said something low-voiced to Jake, then, 'George, please don't just disappear on me. I'm worried about you.'

Always running away, Lyle had accused her. Never letting the people who loved her get close. Where was she going?

'George, where are you going? Can you salvage the boat?'

'No,' she'd answered absently. 'I'm coming to you, if you can put me up for a while.'

The next day she tried to spot Green Island from the sky when the jet was climbing. She lost her bearings as the jet circled and she couldn't tell if the island she fixed on was Green or not.

In Vancouver, she managed to fill the better part of four days with dashing around. It was almost like the days after Scott's death, when she'd torn into desperate activity, refusing to think.

She borrowed Jenny's car and took the ferry to Victoria to see her insurance agent. He glared at her and asked a lot of questions, informed her that this claim would send her rates sky-high if she ever tried to insure a boat again.

In Vancouver, her bank. New cheques applied for, new banking card issued on the spot. She was once more connected to the convenience of modern banking, able to get money anywhere she could find a Bank of Montreal banking machine. New driver's licence. New Mastercard coming in a couple of weeks.

She went shopping. She bought a soft cuddly bear for Robin. The bear had a big bib that bore the words *I love you*. She also bought some Love's Baby Soft perfume and bubble bath. She used Lyle's card for the bear, her own money for the perfume. She packaged them with Lyle's credit card and a cheque for fifty dollars. She sent the whole thing to him by registered mail.

She put a letter to Robin in with the package, giving Jenny's house as her return address. She didn't write to Lyle. She didn't know what to say to him. She wasn't ready to come to terms with Lyle yet. She bought a Walkman for herself and listened to the tape Russ had given her from Lyle. She played it for Jenny and Jake one evening.

'Very professional,' Jake said, sitting up, with that alert look she'd seen on his face when he was caught up in an exciting project.

Jenny was watching him, half smiling. 'You said he was the lightkeeper? What's his name? What does he look like?'

'Lyle. Lyle Stevens.' She thought of one or two of the films Jake and Jenny had done and she added, 'He's very good-looking. Very photogenic, I would imagine.'

Then she moved quickly, because she could see that Jake was interested and she wanted to hold back and think about this. Did Lyle really want her interfering with his life? Did he still want her? Did she want to interfere? It would mean a relationship with Lyle.

When she was seventeen, being in love had meant giving herself up to Scott, letting him enfold her and take control of her life. What did it mean now?

She could have a baby.

She closed her eyes tightly, feeling stirrings within herself, seeing Lyle bent over her, watching a small child with wispy red hair nursing at her breast.

What kind of a mother would she be? What sort of wife to a man like Lyle? Could she be all the things Hazel hadn't been for him?

He wanted more than Scott ever had. Lyle wanted a partner. Intimacy.

She and Scott had never really had intimacy. She'd felt warmth and protectiveness from him, but she'd never given him anything more than her adoration. It was all he'd wanted. He hadn't wanted to know what made her tremble, what made her joyful. And although she'd worshipped him, she'd never seen him as a human man with frailties and fears. She'd thought they had everything.

Lyle wanted more.

Or did he? What if she was reading him wrong? What if he didn't feel any of the things she thought he felt? It was impossible! If she let him get that close—if she let anyone get that close to her—she'd never be safe again. The thought terrified her!

She booked a charter flight to Montreal. Two days later she cancelled it. She made reservations for a flight to Mexico, then inexplicably boarded the ferry to Vancouver Island and went to visit her mother in Campbell River.

She was afraid to run, and afraid to stay. She was terrified of the implications of loving Lyle. The only thing that frightened her more was the thought of never seeing him again.

She stayed for three days, listening to her mother talking about the garden, the neighbours' children who were turning into hooligans as they grew up, and the weekly bridge club.

On the last day of her visit, her mother said suddenly, 'Georgina, I've always wanted to tell you how sorry I was that I opposed your marriage to Scott.'

George was peeling potatoes. She stopped the action of the peeler and stared at her mother. 'That's a long time ago.'

Her mother shrugged. She was small, but George had always felt slightly intimidated by her. Now she said, 'It kept you away from home for a long time. I missed you. And it was your life. I'd no business trying to live it for you.' She took a deep breath, said, 'And I hope you won't be angry with me now, but I don't want you to spend your life like this. You were never meant to live alone. I think you should go out and find a man and——'

She spread her hands wide, indicating somehow the years of her own widowhood. 'You should have a family.'

'Any man?' asked George, smiling, mischief lighting her eyes. 'What should I be looking for?'

'Love,' said her mother.

'I'll think about it,' she promised.

She'd hardly thought about anything else since leaving Green Island. She didn't mention Lyle, but when she left the next day she promised to return soon.

She went to the north end of Vancouver Island. She visited a second-hand bookshop and picked up an armful of books—everything from Agatha Christie to Georgette Heyer. Then she checked into a small motel and spent two weeks walking the beaches and reading. She felt instinctively that if she could bury herself in the books, vegetate for a while, her subconscious might straighten out her tangled emotions.

One afternoon, in the middle of an Agatha Christie murder, it occurred to her that Lyle loved her. Although he hadn't actually said the words, it was in every look he gave her. And Lyle's kind of love wasn't anything like Scott's. Scott had wanted her in spite of her wildness. Scott hadn't loved all of her. He'd loved what he wanted her to be.

Lyle loved the woman who was crazy enough to sail single-handed from Mexico to Alaska at the wrong time of year, the woman who was restless and afraid and prone to argue about anything that seemed to threaten her freedom.

Was she insane? Running from a man who felt like that about her? She called the travel agent and cancelled her Mexico reservations. She took bus and ferry back to Vancouver, arrived at Jenny's in mid-afternoon when the house was empty. They'd bought a big old house on the north shore, overlooking the water. They kept a spare key in the porch, where George suspected any intelligent burglar could find it.

She was feeling a little less sure of herself by the time she opened the door. If Lyle loved her, surely he knew that it was impossible for her to live on a lighthouse. She'd never pretended to liking the isolation, but what if he expected her to——

To be someone else. She was George. He had to accept that. If he really loved her, he would accept that.

She opened the door, found a can of Coke in the refrigerator and walked, sipping the cool liquid, into the living-room. She was wearing blue jeans and an over-sized shirt. She discarded her sandals and went barefoot across the floor.

Her mail was on the mantel, not far from the empty playpen. Her new telephone calling-card. A letter from the insurance agent saying that her claim would be delayed while they waited for the coastguard report on her shipwreck.

An envelope addressed to her in childish printing, with Green Island Lighthouse as the return address. A small package with Lyle's handwriting on it. Not a letter, but another cassette.

Her hands were trembling as she pushed it into the tape deck. The speaker crackled, then Lyle's voice was saying gruffly, 'This one's for you, honey.'

The music filled the room. The drums and the bass guitar. Lyle's voice. 'I use my own voice to show the words,' he'd once said to her, but this was more than words and music. It was a love song, her love song. She sank down on to the hearth rug, hugging her knees and listening to Lyle's voice, Lyle's music, asking her to let him love her.

The music faded to silence. Then there was only the sound of traffic outside...a faint crackling that came from the stereo that Jenny and Jake must have bought at a bargain sale somewhere.

Sitting alone in that big living-room, tears flowing down her cheeks, she admitted to herself that she was waiting for Lyle to come. She'd prided herself on being independent, on knowing her own mind. That was all nonsense! Lyle had touched her heart and she had run, terrified. And now, knowing she couldn't run away from her own heart, she was waiting for him to come. Waiting for him to take the decision out of her hands.

And he wasn't going to do that, damn him!

Here she was, all ready to let him carry her off—mind you, she meant to do a little fighting, to negotiate her own terms, but she fully expected him to come and get her!

And he wasn't going to.

He was going to leave it up to her. He'd sent her his message, his love, and if anyone made the next move it was going to have to be her. All right! But he was asking for it. If he was leaving this up to her, then she was going to do it her way! He'd better love her, really love her, because she was about to interfere in his life unforgivably!

Maybe it wasn't so bad being a volatile, restless woman. If she weren't, who would get Lyle and Robin off that lighthouse?

She grinned, surprised at herself, because she was actually feeling good about herself. Why not? Emotions were better than being cold. And being restless meant you saw more, did more. And so many people loved her. Jenny. Her mother. Robin. And Lyle. She took the cassette out of the stereo. Then she opened Robin's letter.

'Dear George

Uncle Russ and Ant Dorothy had a baby boy. Uncle Russ is coming home in two weeks, but Ant Dorothy is gonna stay in town another month with the baby. The baby is called Lyle for my dad.

We're gonna go on holidays on the fifteenth. We're taking the ferry and visiting my grandma near Victoria. Then we're flying to Vancouver an then I go to the hospital.

Daddy says I shouldn't ask you, but please will you come see me in the hospital like you said? I'm having my opration on May the twentieth.

Love, Robin'

She was still sitting on the rug in front of the fireplace when Jenny came in. Jake was right behind her, the baby in a pack on his back, with its fist clamped on a lock of Jake's hair.

George was frightened inside. It was a delicious, exciting fear, something like taking *Lady Harriet* before a gale, surfing wild before the wind. She stood up and moved quickly towards them, stopping Jenny's surprised greeting with a quick question.

'Jake, doesn't that fellow you introduced me to—Dennis?—doesn't he work at a travel agency? Would he be willing to do you a favour?'

'He does,' Jake agreed, turning to let Jenny lift the baby out of the pack, giving a special smile to his wife and a grin for George. 'And he might. And hello, cousin. Nice to see you back. Changed your mind about going to Mexico?'

'Yes, I have. I never really wanted to go to Mexico.' She was starting to pace the room, wanting action now. 'Do you think he could track down a reservation for me? I need to know the flight someone's arriving on from Victoria.'

'We could do it ourselves,' said Jenny, her eyes alive with curiosity. 'We can use the computer at the studio to get into the airline reservations.'

'Good!' She swung back to them. Jenny was holding the baby in her arms. Jake was half listening to George, but mostly watching his wife and baby. 'And, please, would you two mind awfully if Lyle and his daughter stayed here while they're in Vancouver?'

Of course they didn't mind. They had that big old house, and Jenny was agonisingly curious to see this song-writing lightkeeper. Jake was still grateful to George for helping him and Jenny get together. George noticed that his eyes lost their focus as he thought about a rocky isolated lighthouse with a music man tending the light. It was a natural for a television documentary. Good. If Jake was interested, Jenny would do the rest when she met Lyle. She wasn't quite sure how Lyle would react, but she planned to shake up his comfortable lighthouse life.

The computer at Austin Media co-operated by producing the date, time and flight number for Lyle Stevens's reservation on the Victoria-Vancouver jet.

George felt the excitement growing inside her. The days seemed to drag by as she waited for Lyle to come to Vancouver, then suddenly it was time and she felt her confidence draining away.

She almost ran Jenny's car into a bus on the way to the airport. The driver shouted at her and she had no retort to make at all. She just drove on, trembling. She rushed to the airport, but arrived far too early. Then the plane was delayed ... And she waited.

Ten minutes left until the plane touched down. She couldn't get through security to meet them at the gate. Where should she wait? She mentally retraced the route for disembarking passengers, and decided that the luggage carousels were the best place to wait. They had to come down that escalator and they would surely have luggage to claim.

Maybe this wasn't a good idea, after all. Surprising him. Had she read his feelings wrong? Would he rather she waited, passively, for him to contact her?

Given time to think, had he come to regret writing the song for her? Love was only a word, after all. Not everybody meant the same thing when they said it. She hadn't felt like this when she was a seventeen-year-old girl worshipping the tall man who said he loved her.

A loudspeaker voice announced the arrival of someone's flight. She couldn't hear over the excited babble of a group of teenaged girls wearing school uniforms. Lyle's flight? No! It was too soon. She wasn't ready, after all.

She found the carousel with Lyle's flight number over it. It was turning slowly, still empty. She watched the escalator intently. What if they had only hand luggage? They would go down the escalator and out of the terminal. She could miss them by glancing away.

She should have written to tell him she would meet him.

What if he didn't want her here?

Damn it! Stop it, George! If he loves you, he knows you'd do this sort of thing. He——

She moved to make sure she had an unobstructed view of the escalator. An endless stream of people riding down towards her.

Two lovers holding hands. The girl stumbled as she stepped off the escalator. Her lover caught her in eager arms. Three children with a harried mother. The younger boy poked the older in the ribs, then gazed off innocently. A man with a turban and a long beard. Two tall young men in immaculate suits, carrying briefcases. A girl in jeans with long straight hair, her face worried and intense.

Lyle.

His head was bent, his eyes on the girl beside him. His hand rested on the rail, covering Robin's as they rode down.

His face seemed more lined than she remembered, his eyes narrowed as he glanced around. He didn't see her.

He was wearing a light brown sports jacket over an open-necked shirt. His throat showed bronzed above the open collar, his hair glinting red and curling just slightly over the collar of his jacket.

George tried to make her feet move, to go to them, but she was frozen. God! She was terrified. She just had to walk up and say hello, but she was utterly panic-stricken.

Robin was craning her neck, taking in everything, her face eager but tense. It was Robin who saw George first, just as they stepped off the escalator. She pulled away from Lyle and went flying across the space between them, dodging the two men with briefcases and flinging herself into George's arms.

'I knew you'd come! I knew it! I knew it!'

George staggered back under the weight of Robin's surprisingly solid body. She braced herself on a pillar and let her arms go around the girl, burying her face in the long soft hair and ignoring the elbow that seemed to be pushed hard into her ribs.

Robin felt warm, full of enchanting corners like the point of her elbow. George held her, afraid to look up, trying to put off that moment when she'd meet Lyle's eyes.

Even though she tried to prepare herself, when she looked up at Lyle her heart slammed hard against her ribcage. Surely Robin must feel it?

He was taller than she remembered, his hair sleeker, his eyes a deeper blue. Or was it the clothes he was wearing? She was used to seeing him in jeans, with his hair tousled by the wind. His face was stern, not smiling. He didn't say hello. She had thought she would know how he felt the moment she saw him, but she couldn't read anything in his eyes. Her own smile faded and she tried to make her eyes cool and friendly.

It was long seconds before Robin pulled back and twisted around to her father. 'Daddy, did you know she'd be here?'

He shook his head. His eyes left hers, took in the activity around them. 'Our luggage should be here any minute.' Lyle pointed to the carousel and Robin moved away from them to watch the luggage that was starting to slide down the ramp.

George watched Robin, avoiding Lyle's eyes. She should never have come. He'd known where to find her if he wanted her. She should have waited.

George said, 'She's hardly limping at all today.'

He spoke as if to a stranger. 'She forgets to favour the leg when she's excited. And it is almost normal now. This is the last time she'll have to have surgery. Then— exercises and time. This time next year she could be running and jumping.' He pushed his hands in the pockets of his elegant trousers, seeming to turn away from her. 'Why are you here, George? For my daughter?'

She let the pillar behind her take her weight again. She closed her eyes briefly, wished she could be somewhere else. She said, 'No, not just for Robin.'

Robin was shifting from foot to foot, craning her neck to see each piece of luggage as it started down the ramp to the carousel. Lyle was facing her now. The ice had left his eyes. She thought she could see love there, but she wasn't sure.

'Lyle, I'm——' She broke off and laughed nervously. 'I'm kind of scared.'

'What of?' He leaned one arm on the post above her head. He was very close now, only inches away. Why was he making this so hard for her? Why couldn't he just look at her and know? Did there have to be words?

'You. Me.' She touched his immaculate jacket fleetingly. 'You and me. And you look so formal, I don't quite know what to say to you.'

His eyebrow quirked up. 'Formal? I'm not exactly in tie and tails, you know.'

'No. And you're not in blue jeans.' She was getting her breathing under control. She had to. He was controlled, and she had to be controlled, too.

'You're beautiful,' he said, his voice suddenly ragged. 'And if you're scared, would it help to know that I'm terrified?'

'Yes,' she whispered, moving closer. He couldn't possibly have heard her with all the noise around, but he smiled, then he frowned.

'George.' His arms gripped her shoulders suddenly. She was half-way into his arms, then he stopped and warned, 'Be careful. Don't let me push you into anything.'

She met his eyes, seeing a strong-willed man holding himself back. 'Be careful yourself,' she warned, a smile growing on her lips. 'I might be the one doing the pushing.'

She was glad to see him laugh, the light reaching his eyes. 'I guess I can hold my own, honey.' His lips were on hers in a hot, fleeting caress. 'And if I can't, I'm sure I'll enjoy losing.'

Then he was cool and remote, collecting his luggage, steering Robin towards the exit, letting George keep up with them on her own. How could he be so casual? She was jelly inside, and he was managing luggage, as if it were the most important thing in the world.

'A taxi,' Lyle said, looking across at the line-up of various taxis waiting for fares.

'I've got a car,' George offered, not taking his arm because he didn't seem to be offering it. 'I brought Jenny's car.'

When they were in the small car, Lyle at her side and Robin in the back seat, George started the engine and let it run for a minute. Jenny's car had a disconcerting habit of stalling dead if you tried to put it in motion too soon.

'How are your parents, Lyle?'

'They're fine. Did Robin tell you we were going to visit them?'

She nodded, then said, 'Jenny and Jake would like you and Robin to stay at their place while you're in Vancouver. They've got this big old house that they rattle around in.'

'Why? Why do they want us?'

'Because——' She pushed the car into gear. She couldn't say, 'Because I love you.' She would never have imagined he could be so hard to talk to. Was he being deliberately difficult?

He said, 'We're probably better to stay at the hotel. It's handy for the hospital—only a few blocks away.' He shifted, laid his arm along the back of the seat. His hand was only an inch from her shoulder. He glanced back at Robin.

George carefully manoeuvred the car out of the car park. 'They've invited you because I asked them to. They're my family and they're—well, they're grateful that you pulled me out of the ocean. They want to meet you.'

She was a coward. Why didn't she say it? *They've invited you because you're important to me. Because I asked them to, and they're blind if they don't know I love you.*

He shifted again. She guessed that he'd be happier if he were at the wheel of this car. She said defensively, 'I'm a good driver.'

'I don't doubt it,' he said mildly, making her irrationally angry. Anger was easier than this vulnerable uncertainty, and she took refuge in it for a moment.

Robin was too busy staring out of the window to say a word. The inside of the car was silent until they were working their way through the traffic down Granville Street. When George couldn't stand the silence any more, she asked, 'Did you enjoy visiting your parents?'

'Yes.' He shifted to watch her. His voice sounded too patient, as if he were humouring her. 'I told you they're living a few miles outside Victoria? They've got a couple of acres and two big dogs.' He smiled then, and his voice deepened. 'The dogs are *very* big. Robin was trying to ride one of them.'

'It sounds nice.' She made herself keep her eyes on the road. She'd never forgive herself if she had an accident driving Lyle. She didn't know why she said, 'I visited my mother in Campbell River.'

'How is she?' He sounded as if he were asking about an old acquaintance.

'OK.' She shifted gears as the truck ahead of her slowed. Why didn't Jenny get a car with an automatic transmission? 'She told me she was sorry she went against

me when I wanted to marry Scott.' He didn't say anything. She could feel him watching her. 'She said I should
find another man and get married again.' Her eyes
flickered to the rear-view mirror, but Robin was staring
at the driver of an eighteen-wheel rig beside them. What
would he say? It was almost an invitation, bringing up
the idea of her remarrying.

Lyle looked away from her, his voice tense as he said
bluntly, 'My mother's been talking to Hazel, my ex-wife.
She wants me to see her.' He cleared his throat. 'She's
hoping we'll get back together.'

Had he really said that?

She searched his face and found it so remote that she
believed he might be thinking of getting back with Hazel.
If she could see his eyes, she might know for sure, but
he was looking away. Why had he sent her the song, if
he felt like that? Had she made a mistake, thinking he
still wanted her? No, she remembered his eyes at the
airport, and knew that he hadn't stopped wanting her,
but maybe it was only desire, not love.

She'd mentioned marriage. Was that why he'd brought
up the subject of Hazel? Had he ever mentioned
marriage?

No.

God! She was stupid! She hadn't thought for even a
moment that he wanted only an affair. He'd invited her
to stay at the lighthouse, or to come back later. What
did that mean? A woman named Cynthia had once
stayed. Now she was gone.

Had he written a song for her, too? Well, George
wasn't a Cynthia! She wasn't for casual taking and
casting off! She was——

She wasn't his wife. To have and to hold. Till death
do us part. Scott was gone for ever, but perhaps Hazel
wasn't. Hazel could come back.

They went the rest of the way in silence. Thankfully,
at the big old Austin house, there was the noise of Jake

and Jenny and Mandy, the baby, to cover the fact that George didn't know what to say to Lyle. And Lyle seemed to have nothing to say to George.

Robin loved Jenny's baby. She begged Jenny to let her feed Mandy, then she had Jenny showing her how to burp the baby.

'She needs changing,' said Jenny when Mandy started fussing again.

Robin's eyes lit up. 'I'll do it—if you'll show me how.'

Jake had been pacing the floor, explaining some new project to Lyle. Now he turned his black eyes on Robin. 'I'll have to show you the diapering, Robin. Jenny and I made a deal when Amanda was born. We split the work of parenting this baby, but since I'm not equipped to feed her, I get to do the diapers.'

He pushed his hand through a lock of black hair, then reached down to take the baby in one arm. He offered the other hand to Robin and the three of them wandered off into the back of the house somewhere.

Lyle caught Jenny's eye. He said quietly, 'Thank you for having us. She was going to spend the evening having nerves about going into the hospital tomorrow.'

'She's a lovely girl,' said Jenny, pushing back her shoulder-length brown hair. She was growing it long and it was at an in-between stage right now. She smiled at Lyle. 'Now tell me about what happened to my wild cousin up there on your island. All she'll say is that she ran her boat aground.'

George stood up and moved to the window. 'That's all I remember, Jenny. *Lady Harriet* hit the rocks, then I hit the water.' She turned and found Lyle looking at her for the first time since they arrived. Their eyes held.

'It was just luck that I found her,' said Lyle, his voice dropping to a harsh tone. 'It was a stormy day. Visibility was terrible. I was inside, working on a song. In that kind of weather I usually stay inside, just poking my head out the door to get the sky and sea conditions for my weather reports.'

George sank down into a chair, listening for the first time to a blow-by-blow description of her rescue. She remembered the wild water, the storm, and realised that Lyle was right. It was only luck that she had survived for him to pull from the sea.

George couldn't help smiling as Jenny did her magic with those quiet questions of hers. She wanted background on Lyle, and he hadn't a chance against her warm interest.

'My mother was a concert pianist before she met my father,' he told them. 'She tried to teach me, but my fingers wouldn't do what hers would. I could hear the sounds in my mind, but my fingers wouldn't bring them to life.' He smiled at George, said, 'I tried guitar, but it was the same. I never had the kind of touch George has with a guitar. Then I discovered synthesisers. They started using computer chips in music just for people like me.'

'You should see the set-up he has.' George sat forward to free her arms for descriptive gestures. 'It's in the basement. Totally carpeted with thick carpeting for sound-proofing—I do mean completely! Carpet on the floor, the walls. Sound-proofing tiles on the ceiling. The windows blanketed.'

'To keep the noise from getting out?' speculated Jenny.

Jake caught the last part of their conversation as he came back into the room. 'No,' he corrected his wife as he set Mandy down into the playpen near the fireplace. 'To keep outside noises from getting in, just like keeping light out of a photo lab.'

'That's right,' Lyle agreed. 'A recording can be ruined by noises you'd never hear with your ear.'

Robin picked up a rattle and waved it slowly in front of the baby's eyes.

Jake asked, 'How do you manage to turn one man into a five-piece band with vocal?'

'The vocal is simple,' said Lyle with a grin. 'I pull shipwrecked maidens out of the water and force them to sing for their supper. The five-piece band just takes a good synthesiser and a multi-track recorder.'

That got Lyle and Jake into the technical aspects of a one-man sound studio. George went to get the tape of the song she and Lyle had recorded together. She put it on the recorder and turned the volume low. Robin recognised the music and looked up to smile at George. Lyle and Jake were too deeply involved in conversation to notice, but Jenny's eyes went dreamy as she swayed to the music, looking at Lyle. Jake fell silent, staring at his wife.

'Think of it,' Jenny said softly. 'A rocky island, windswept. Gulls flying overhead, an eagle. There are eagles, aren't there? Spray breaking over the rocks, and inside—the sounds of music. We orchestrate the whole thing with his music. Jake, you can get some fantastic shots with the camera. Inside and outside. Sea and music. Tremendous contrasts.' She frowned, said slowly, 'What about market?'

Jake started prowling, a sure sign that he was sold on the idea. 'I bet one of the networks would take it. I'll talk to Brady. Maybe even prime-time. One of those human interest shows—how about Brenda Lake's show?'

She'd known it would be like this. If Jake and Jenny met Lyle, and heard his music, they'd catch fire at the idea of turning the music-making lightkeeper into a film.

But what about Lyle. He was silent, stern. Was he angry? George slipped away to make coffee in the kitchen. She filled the filter-maker with water, got out the coffee, then turned for the filters and found Lyle leaning against the doorway watching her.

'You planned this idea of a documentary.'

She shook her head, smiling. 'Jenny and Jake are planning it. You saw it happen yourself, the birth of an idea.'

He shrugged. 'That may be, but you set it up.'

She had never been able to pretend with Lyle. Instinctively, he knew her too well. A mischievous sparkle flashed over her face.

'If you put good material in front of Jenny, she starts thinking, planning. Then she starts talking, and if she paints word-pictures that Jake can see through his camera lens—then you've got an Austin media documentary. They're quite a team, you know.'

Her smile faded when it didn't get an answer.

'Why did you do it?' he asked harshly.

He'd sent her a love song, as if the next move was hers, but his mother wanted him to see his ex-wife again. Why had he told her that?

'I—wanted you to have some other choices.' This was a terrible mistake, trying to manipulate him. How could she admit the truth, that she'd wanted to give him a way off the lights? That she'd been offering herself as bait if he would leave the lighthouse.

'Other than what?' His voice was clipped, his eyes icy cold.

'Other than living on a lighthouse,' she said desperately. 'You said it was for Robin, so you could be near her and still—if you let them do this film, it could help with your songs. The publicity...'

'I'm aware of the value of publicity,' he grated. He moved and she found herself moving closer to him, inviting his touch, until she realised that he was stepping back from her. What was he doing? Why was he keeping her at a distance? She didn't want to love him like this if he wasn't going to want her! In his song he'd asked her to love him.

'Daddy?' Robin was tugging gently at Lyle's hand. 'Jenny wants to know if I want to sleep in a room with the baby, or if I want a room for myself. Is it OK if I sleep in Mandy's room?'

CHAPTER NINE

LYLE wouldn't stay there a second night.

'It's too far from the hospital,' he would say. He'd make it sound convincing. The truth was that he had to get away from George. She was so close, so damned desirable. She seemed to be sending him messages that she was willing.

But willing for what?

He loved her with such a terrible intensity that it frightened him, yet he dared not move closer and take her in his arms. What did she want? An affair? Just a man in her bed?

God, that would be ironic! Last year, he'd met Cynthia McLeod and let her talk her way on to the island, into his bed, mostly because he wanted someone warm and willing. It could have been anyone, though Cynthia had tried to make him love her. She'd finally given up, left—minus that damned Kitimat shirt.

He'd felt guilty about Cynthia loving him; felt relieved when she married a fisherman from Prince Rupert. Was that what he would be to George? The lover she felt guilty about discarding?

George hadn't reacted at all when he told her that his mother was promoting a reconciliation with Hazel. If she cared anything about him, surely that would have upset her? It had shaken him badly when his mother came out with that. He had made sure that she knew, in no uncertain terms, that Hazel was the *last* woman he'd ever want.

He wanted George.

And she wanted him to do a documentary. What the hell did she mean by saying she wanted him to have more choices? Why?

He didn't sleep all night. He was in the guest bedroom, on the top floor of the Austin house. George was two doors away. If he got up and walked down that hall, knocked softly on her door, would she open the door for him?

He thought she would. He thought that she would let him make love to her. It wouldn't be like the night in the basement of his lighthouse home, when he'd had to draw back from the edges of ecstasy. He was prepared this time. There would be no child as the result of their union of passion.

'I'll have your child,' she had whispered. 'Give me your child, Lyle.'

He tried to fight down the wild surge of desire that came every time he thought about making love to her. He tried vainly to relax his rigid body on the cold sheets. His skin burned with the memory of her body, soft and willing under him. He felt the sting of her fingers digging into him as she shuddered with desire.

I'll have your child. She had meant it, too. She would have his child, but not with him. She'd accept his passion, the seed of his loins, but not his love. He shivered and pulled the blanket up higher. He could see her rearing the child alone, disappearing on him, gone to some crazy spot on the other side of the world. He cursed the poor heating in this old house, yet he knew it would have been warm enough if he weren't going mad with wanting her.

An affair. He'd seen it in her eyes on the lighthouse. Damn! He almost laughed at himself, resenting being wanted just for his body. That was the man's role, wasn't it? Seduce the fair lady—and, by God, she was fair!— and walk away when he'd had his way with her. She was the one who wanted to walk away.

When he heard the house stirring, he got up and went into the shower, turning the water cold and letting it pound on his back while he cursed himself for not going to her the night before. He cut himself twice while shaving, slapped stinging aftershave on the cuts. He almost ran into George when he stepped out of the bathroom.

She was in bare feet, just smothering a yawn. She stared up at him, blinking, her eyes sleepy and vulnerable.

She was wearing a short blue dressing-gown that flowed loose around her. Her face was marked from the sheet she'd been lying on. He touched the red line on her cheek.

'You shouldn't sleep on your stomach.' He wanted to pull her into his arms and feel her softness pressing against him. 'You get sheet marks on your face, and you'll get a sore neck.'

'I know,' she said simply, staring up at him. Once she was dressed and awake she would lose that soft, vulnerable look. It was the look she'd had when he'd been kissing her, touching her.

'Are you wearing anything under that dressing-gown?'

'No.' He saw her breath quicken, her eyes widen.

He couldn't stop himself from touching her, taking her shoulders in his hands and pulling her close until his lips covered hers. She gasped, her breath fanning his lips. Her soft unconfined breasts pressed against the muscles of his chest. He slipped his arms around to her back.

George's arms went up, her fingers tangling in his hair, pulling his head down into a deeper kiss. He let his hands explore her back, shaping her woman's curves close to him, caressing the wonderful contours of her back...down...down until his hands held the excitingly round curve of her buttocks.

Close by, a floorboard creaked.

'Robin,' he groaned, stiffening. He could feel every beautiful inch of George pressing against him. He couldn't bear to let her go.

'No,' she murmured against his lips. 'Robin's downstairs, helping Jenny feed Mandy. It'll be Jake, and he'll probably want the shower.'

'Darling,' he whispered, finding her soft neck with his lips. 'I wish I'd come last night.' He felt her skin quiver from his touch, heard her gasp softly at the pictures his words evoked.

'Did you want me last night, George?'

Her fingers tightened in his hair, then drifted down to his neck, his shoulders. 'Yes...I waited for you to come.'

He let his hands feel the shape of her. The thrust of her hipbones. Her narrow waist. His hands drifted over a trembling softness that was her abdomen, up to grasp the swollen fullness of her breasts through the thick fabric.

'I want to touch you, feel you,' he growled. His fingers fumbled with the button at the front of her gown, slipping inside to touch her hot flesh.

She shuddered and sagged against him. 'Lyle, please!' His fingers found the rigid peak and grasped it gently. 'Oh...'

A door opening, then closing. He stiffened. His hand moved outside the fabric. His voice was tight as he said, 'I've got rotten timing, honey.' His arms gentled, stroking her as if he could ease the tension he'd imparted to her aching body.

'You sure have!' Jake's voice, vibrant and laughing, followed by Jake himself in jeans and bare chest. Tactfully, his eyes just glanced off them, then moved on. 'Excuse me, you two, but if I could just get past? Into the shower? Then you can resume whatever you were doing.'

George jerked back, hugging her gown to herself, not realising that she was revealing the aroused curves of her body by pulling the fabric tight against her skin.

Jake laughed gently, patting her shoulder as he went past. 'Your turn, is it?' he asked teasingly. George had a sudden vivid memory of Jake standing on the pontoon of a seaplane, shouting his love across to Jenny on the deck of *Lady Harriet*.

'What did he mean by that?' Lyle had his breathing under control now. Well, almost. 'I'd better get downstairs,' he decided. 'Robin——'

George asked suddenly, 'Are you going to see your wife?'

'She's not my wife,' he said harshly. 'We're divorced. Years ago.'

George shivered and pulled the gown tighter. If he felt that strongly about Hazel, he might be fooling himself thinking he didn't still love her. 'She still has the power to upset you, it seems.'

'That's for damned sure,' he muttered. 'I don't know why the hell she'd want to see me now.' He added wryly, 'I wish you weren't so bloody good-natured and understanding about it. It's hard on my ego—what did you say?'

'You heard,' she muttered. She wanted to tear the woman off the face of the earth. It wasn't as if she'd ever made him happy, but she was causing trouble even now. 'It was a very unladylike comment. And I'm anything but understanding. I don't understand anything! If you want her back, why are you kissing me? And——'

'And?' he prompted, feeling hope rising in him until suddenly the fire closed down in her eyes and she was gone, back into her bedroom.

Damn!

Downstairs, Jenny was efficiently dishing out bacon and eggs while Robin spooned baby food into Mandy's mouth and all over her face. Lyle accepted a cup of coffee and watched his daughter, wishing he could give her a mother—George—and a baby sister. Damn, who was he fooling? He wanted George for himself, in his arms and his life and his home. Wherever the hell she wanted to be, but near him. And a baby. Two babies.

Jake came down and gave Jenny a kiss before he accepted his coffee.

Robin asked, 'Do you have a baby-sitter?'

Jake shook his head. 'But we'll have to get one soon. Once Mandy starts walking it won't be possible to have her with us at the studio. But, for the moment, she's nice to have around.'

Jenny wiped baby food from the baby's cheeks. 'We have a friend—Monica—who runs a day-care centre. Mandy goes there when we can't have her with us.'

Robin took a sip from her glass of orange juice. Lyle noticed that she hadn't eaten any of her own breakfast. He recognised the nervous tension in her eyes from past visits to the hospital.

He said, 'I think Robin would like to run a day-care centre. She likes babies.' The distraction worked. Robin's eyes lit up and she started asking quick questions about the unknown Monica and her fascinating job.

'I'll take you to see her,' offered Jenny, 'after you get out of hospital.'

Two cups of coffee helped make him feel more alert, but he knew his lack of sleep would catch up with him soon.

George came in, sparkling fresh in a flowered summer skirt and a thin embroidered blouse. She looked wonderful, but she wouldn't meet his eyes.

Jenny said, 'We're just going off to work. Lyle, you and Robin make yourselves at home.'

That was when he announced, 'Thanks, Jenny, but we'll be leaving in a bit. Robin's checking into the hospital this afternoon, and I'll move to the hotel.'

George wouldn't meet his eyes. He should have talked to her first, not made the announcement cold without her knowing. Robin said tensely, 'George, will you visit me?'

Her voice was falsely bright. 'Sure, Robin. Just tell me what time and I'll be there.'

George watched Lyle and Robin drive away in a yellow cab. Some independent woman she was! Emancipated, hell! She hadn't even got the nerve to tell him she loved him. She was terribly afraid that he'd changed his mind, that his love song had been a thing of the moment.

Why hadn't he come to her last night? Well, for that matter, why hadn't she gone to him? Simple. She'd been afraid.

Maybe he was afraid, too.

She certainly hadn't given him any reason to feel sure of her. She hadn't told him that she loved him. She hadn't told him that he'd made her feel whole for the first time in her life. She hadn't said that she even wanted to cook his breakfasts—well, some of the time, anyway—and she wanted to make a child with him, to be a mother to Robin and to their children. They could be grand-parents together.

In the song, he'd said he loved her.

This was crazy! There was nothing she could do right now. She tried to push aside her thoughts and set to work cleaning Jenny's house.

She wished she could have gone with Lyle and Robin. Surely it would have helped Lyle to have someone else there to distract Robin from her nervousness about the surgery. Why hadn't he asked her to come?

She rubbed hard at a spot on the coffee table.

Funny, she'd always thought she was a direct and forthright person. If she wanted to go with Lyle, why hadn't she said, 'Can I come with you?'

She'd been doing that all her adult life. She'd resented Scott's attitude to her music, but she had never said,

'Scott, music is important to me. My soul needs music, and it doesn't make me love you any less.'

Lyle, I love you. Would it be enough, to say that? He was being so strange, reaching out to her, then drawing back. Was it possible that he still loved the woman who had once been his wife?

He'd written the song for George, his stray lady.

She wanted to go out walking, but she was afraid Lyle might telephone and she would miss the call. She hadn't given him the number. Had he looked at the phone and written it down? It was in the telephone book, but what if he forgot Jake's last name? Jake Austin. There was no reason for him to remember that.

She had hoped he would want to do the documentary with Jake and Jenny. It would almost inevitably give his songs a boost, give him a way to make his living in the city, make it possible for her to live with him.

She'd even live on a lighthouse if he really wanted that. It sounded like a trap, but it hadn't felt like one when he held her in his arms. There had been the ocean and the beach. The music-room. He had a plane that he brought out in the summers. They could fly everywhere, be free to move about.

There were neighbours. Russ might smile at her again if she came back with Lyle. His wife, Dorothy, was almost certainly a nice woman. She'd like to see their new baby, the baby named Lyle.

What was she going to do if Lyle didn't want her?

The phone didn't ring. In the afternoon she called the hospital to ask about visiting hours. She thought Lyle might call her, suggest they visit Robin together. He didn't call.

She went to the hospital near the end of the evening visiting hours. She found Robin half-asleep, and alone.

'Daddy was here a minute ago,' she mumbled. 'I didn't get any dinner, and they gave me a sleepy pill.'

Her eyes drooped and she was asleep.

Lyle was very close by. She could walk to his hotel in minutes, see him. But if he wanted to see her, wouldn't he call her? Was she asking for too much, assuming too much? She shouldn't have mentioned marriage. That had been her mistake. If he wanted an affair——

It didn't matter what he wanted. She'd be whatever he wanted——

No, she wouldn't! She'd finished with that. She was herself, George, faults and all.

And she loved him.

She went home. Twice she almost told the taxi driver to turn back, but in the end she arrived at Jenny and Jake's home. She went to bed early and spent a sleepless night. What would he do if she called him in the middle of the night? No. Tonight belonged to Robin. Tomorrow she'd have her surgery, and until that was over she couldn't expect Lyle to have any time for anyone but his daughter.

Then, if he wanted an affair, they'd have an affair. She'd take whatever loving he could give her. If he wanted the lighthouse, than George would go with him. She'd have to be honest with him, tell him she didn't know how long she could live out there, but she'd try it.

By mid-afternoon the next day she knew that she couldn't stand waiting any longer. She'd always been terrible at waiting.

She left Jenny's house, went to the corner shop, looking for a book to read, picked up a romance, knowing she couldn't read it without thinking of Lyle. Then she ran back, imagining the phone ringing in an empty house. It started ringing as she was fumbling for the key in Jenny's porch. She dropped the key. When she bent to pick it up, her bag disgorged its contents on to the floor.

Damn! Wallet and lipstick all over. A scattering of odds and ends of useless paper. A few pennies. She left the mess and shoved the key into the lock. It stuck. She forgot for a minute that you had to hold up the door for the key to turn smoothly. Why couldn't Jenny and Jake have a house without these temperamental problems? She tripped on the rug inside the door, landing flat on her stomach with her hands taking a stinging slap against the linoleum.

The telephone stopped ringing. She got to it finally, picked it up. She heard the howl of the dialling tone in her ear. It had probably been Jenny, checking on plans for supper. Or the operator, checking the line.

What if he didn't phone again? What if he had called her, and never tried again? What if he'd called with bad news about Robin?

She fumbled for the telephone book, searched desperately for the Holiday Inn.

It rang again, a shrill sound. She jerked it up quickly.

'Hello?'

'Hi, honey.' He sounded very close. She could feel his breath in her ear.

'Did you call a minute ago?'

'Yes. I thought I had the wrong number.'

She shifted the receiver. Her fingers gripped it tightly. It was going to be all right. He'd called. And Robin was all right. She knew from his voice that it was all right. 'I was outside. I went to the shop.' She glanced back at the open door. She hadn't picked up the mess from her bag. 'I couldn't get the damned key to work in the lock. When I got to the phone, you were gone... Where are you? How did Robin's surgery go?'

She could hear sounds with his voice. A radio? People? 'The hotel. I just left Robin at the hospital. She had her surgery. She was in the recovery-room, groggy and mostly asleep. The doctor says it went perfectly, that after six months of physiotherapy she won't know which leg had the limp.'

'Does she know? Did you tell her?'

'I told her, but she may not remember. She's still pretty much under the anaesthetic.'

She sat down cross-legged on the floor, her hand flying out to stop the telephone from crashing to the floor when she pulled the cord tight. 'How long will she be in the hospital?'

'About a week. She's sharing a room with another girl who's having surgery on her knee in the morning. They were comparing legs this morning as they wheeled Robin out for her surgery.'

'It'll help her, having someone to talk to.' She wished she could see him. She wished she could touch him, because he'd be tired now, emotionally exhausted. She said, 'I wish I'd been with you.'

'George, I—will you have dinner with me?'

'When?' She glanced down at herself, decided the skirt and blouse would do for anywhere short of a formal high-class dining-room. 'I could come to you now.'

'Yes, now. I'll pick you up.'

She thought of sitting here, waiting for his taxi to drive up outside.

'I'll come to you,' she decided. She didn't want to have to wait.

'Let's meet in the dining-room here. We don't have all that long before visiting hours at the hospital. I'll order for us...and...George, I want more than dinner.'

She wanted to answer, but the words couldn't seem to squeeze past the lump in her throat.

He did love her. He'd always loved her. She had to learn to have confidence in that.

She called the taxi. Did she have time to change before it came? No. The taxi firm had said five minutes. She ran a comb through her hair, put lipstick on her lips. At the last moment she thought to leave a note for Jenny.

'Having dinner with Lyle, then visiting Robin in hospital. George.' She looked at it, then picked up the pen again and added, 'Don't be surprised if I'm late.'

I might not come home at all tonight, she thought, hugging the words to herself like a promise.

The taxi drove up just as she closed the door of the house behind herself. The ride to the Holiday Inn seemed to take for ever.

She came into the dining-room with her eyes searching for him. Instinctively she looked for the table where she'd seen him the night she dined here with Jenny. Over a year ago, and he'd been sitting right there.

He *was* there. He'd already seen her. She walked towards him, very conscious of the way her hips were swaying, of the feel of the fabric sliding over her legs. She could see herself in his eyes. For the first time, she realised that she was an exciting woman.

Not restless and immature, she told herself gaily. Exciting!

'Do you know how beautiful you are?' he asked as he stood behind her, pulling out the chair for her to sit.

'Only when you look at me like that,' she whispered. The waiter was at Lyle's shoulder, a twinkle in his eye as if he'd heard their whispered words.

Lyle had ordered a light wine for her. She held her hands around the glass, sipping, looking around. She could feel his eyes on her.

'You were sitting over there the last time we were here.' He was following her eyes.

'Yes.' She wasn't quite ready to look at him, although her nervousness was mixed with an excitement that made it delicious. 'Jenny was with me. She told me you were watching me.' She'd been very aware of him that evening, trying to pretend she couldn't feel his eyes. Now she said abruptly, 'Would you please tell me about Hazel?'

The waiter leaned over the table, setting steaming bowls of soup down. 'New England clam chowder,' he announced as he set George's bowl down. 'I hope you enjoy it, madam.'

Lyle asked her, 'What's wrong?'

She picked up her spoon, then shook her head and set it down carefully. 'I'm sorry, but I just can't eat clams.'

He lifted his spoon, his lips pursing as he took some of the hot broth into his mouth. 'It's very good. Why don't you try it?' His mouth curved in a lazy smile. 'I wouldn't have thought you'd be squeamish about seafood.'

She pushed the bowl aside and he suddenly realised. 'Your bout with Red Tide?' He caught her hand, his callused fingers curving around hers. 'Remind me to thank Jake when I see him again. I liked him, but I'd forgotten I had him to thank for your being alive... Honey, do we really have to talk about Hazel? I'd much rather talk about you.'

His hand was large and strong, engulfing hers. Over his deep blue eyes, the brows were thick and tangled. Her eyes found a couple of long grey hairs mixed in with the rest.

'You were the one who brought her up—yesterday. And I've been scared ever since.' She pulled at her hand, but his grip tightened.

His hand tightened on hers momentarily. 'Then I'd better talk about her. Honey, she's no threat to you. I don't know—thinking back, I can't imagine how I ever came to be married to her.'

He grinned slowly, his thumb stroking the back of her hand. 'No, that's not quite true. I was flying for a helicopter charter company in the north. I was away from my family and friends, in a strange place. Working a lot of overtime. I hadn't much time for developing a social life, and—well, I was missing the company of women. Then I met Hazel at a party and—it was probably more lust than anything else, but settling down seemed like a good idea.'

He stopped talking. She waited, watching the memories playing over his face. She wasn't frightened any more. Later, he would tell her that he loved her. He'd stopped talking, so she said, 'And so you got married?'

He nodded. 'The fights started before the wedding. That should have warned me, but I was too stupid to realise. I don't mean arguments.' He grinned. 'With you and me, the sparks are part of it all. With Hazel, the arguments were a total communications failure. I can't think of anything we had in common. After the first while, the physical thing wasn't really all that great either.' His fingers were very soft on her hand. 'I think it takes love to make a really good sex life, and we weren't in love. It was mostly war.'

She curled her fingers around his, feeling the stiff hairs at the back of his hand. 'What did you fight about?'

'Everything. She wanted to leave the north. I didn't. She wanted me to apply for a job in California. I don't know why I refused. I don't know if I could have found a flying job there, but I didn't even try.' He shrugged and she could feel his bewildered frustration. 'George, somehow she seemed to bring out the worst in me. If she wanted something, I didn't want it. If she didn't, I did. Music—she hated my spending time on writing songs. She was furious when I bought the synthesiser. She wanted a trip to Europe. In the middle of one screaming fight, she took a hammer to my speakers. I don't know how the hell I managed not to hit her that time.

'I never did hit her, but by the time it was over I could understand how a man could come to striking a woman. Usually I walked out when we fought. In the end I came back from one of those three-day flying charters and found her gone. She'd left Robin with the baby-sitter and told them both she wasn't going to come back. She told Robin she was sick of being mother to a kid with a gimpy leg, and wife to a husband that didn't give a damn about her.'

His hands were tight on hers, hurting. She wanted to hold him in her arms, but she couldn't with all these people around.

'I'm not proud of my part of it,' he went on slowly. 'It hurt Robin terribly. She must have heard a lot of the fighting. I surely did my part in that. I was no better a husband to Hazel than she was a wife to me. If I loved her in the beginning—and I doubt that I did—I surely didn't love her in the end. The only good thing that came out of it was Robin. But it's Robin that makes me frightened of seeing Hazel again. I can't believe she has any love for her daughter, and I don't want Robin hurt again.'

Lyle stopped talking, either because the waiter appeared to take the soup away, or because there was no more to say.

Their dinners would appear in a moment. She wasn't hungry. Lyle hadn't touched his soup. George had a horrible premonition that they would sit over dinner, close, yet separated by their mutual uncertainties. Then they'd go to visit Robin, still with the barriers between them.

She should tell him she loved him, but she couldn't get the words out. She could feel the tension rising in her, was frightened she might say the wrong thing. She saw his eyes, saw him putting up barriers between them in the aftermath of his confidences about his disastrous marriage.

'Can we go?' she asked tightly.

He raised one thick eyebrow. 'Dinner's just coming?' He made it a question.

The waiter was coming. Whatever he was carrying, she couldn't eat it. 'Can we please go—I—oh, damn!' She swallowed. 'I love you, Lyle. Will you please get us out of here?'

His voice was harsh. 'What did you say?'

'Your dinner, sir . . . madam.' The waiter deposited the plates in front of them with a flourish.

Lyle stared at the turkey in front of him. 'I'm sorry. I——' He looked up into the waiter's curious face. 'We have an urgent—ah—we have to go. Right away. If you could bring the bill?' Lyle's face flushed darkly.

The waiter was frowning at the heaped plates. 'Sir, if you——'

'Oh, hell!' Lyle said explosively. He met George's eyes and they both started to laugh. The elderly woman at the table behind him craned around to stare. George got up quickly. Lyle caught her hand.

'See what you started,' he growled.

'I'm sorry.' She met the eyes of the woman at the other table. The woman was listening eagerly. George said, 'I'm not sorry, really, but I *am* sorry about the dinner.' She smiled nervously at the waiter. 'We'll come back another time, I promise. But right now we do have to leave. Could you just charge the bill to his room?'

'Lady,' Lyle murmured in her ear as he pulled her into the elevator, 'you are going to be trouble.' They were alone finally. He pulled her hard against his chest and glowered down at her.

She admitted, 'I've spent my life getting into scrapes. Do you think you can handle that?'

'Getting you out of trouble?' The elevator door opened and he took her hand and led her across the hallway.

He opened the door for her, his hand still holding hers. 'George, where's your ring?'

She stared down at the white band where her wedding ring had been. Till death us do part, she thought.

The memory seemed like a story she had once read. A pleasant story, warm, but not real any more.

'I put the ring away.' She pulled her hand away self-consciously, adding abruptly, 'It's a wedding ring, and I'm not married any more.'

She swept away from him, through the door and towards the window. 'And you don't need to help me get out of scrapes. I usually seem to land on my feet—

more or less. I just thought I should warn you that
I'm——'

'Volatile?' he suggested, smiling. He leaned against
the door, watching her move restlessly towards the
window, then swing back to look at him.

'Do you mind?' she asked, frowning at him.

'Honey, you're gorgeous! Come here.'

She stared out of the window. It was starting to rain
outside. She was thirty years old. How could she be so
incredibly shy?

She said uncertainly, 'You wrote that song for me?'

He nodded, but she wasn't looking. She said, 'I'm
sorry about you and Hazel. I hate thinking of——'

Exasperated, he said, 'George, shut up and come
here!'

She swung around. He wasn't smiling any longer.
'Come here and let me kiss you.'

She was frozen, eyes wide. He looked so confident.
Did he know how good he looked, leaning back, the
smooth fabric of his trousers pulled tight over his thighs?
He shifted, took a step towards her. His hands were at
his sides, fingers spread, just touching his thighs.

Nervously, she stepped back. She felt the cool night
air from the window on her neck.

'George,' he said warningly. 'Why did we come up
here? Because you're sorry about Hazel? Or because you
want to go to bed with me?'

She gasped and swung away.

'Oh, hell! George——' Then he was across the room,
his hands on her shoulders.

She jerked to pull away from him. She said wildly,
'Let go of me! I don't need you! I don't need anyone!'

His lips found hers, smothering the wild protests. 'I
think you do,' he said softly. 'I hope you do, darling.'

She shuddered. His hands were on her shoulders. She
leaned her forehead against his shoulder. 'I'm sorry,'
she whispered.

'Lady, stop talking!' His lips covered hers, smothering the sound, then withdrawing. His arms slipped down and cradled her against him. Still holding her close, he walked them back to a large overstuffed sofa and sank down on it with her held against his chest.

'Is that better?' he asked, feeling her head against his chest. He smoothed back the curls, his fingers feeling the contours of her head through the soft crown of golden hair.

She wiggled, pushing closer into his arms. 'You're not much bigger than Robin,' he said softly, his hand settling on the curve of her hip.

She pushed closer. 'It's not a father I'm looking for.'

He let his fingers explore the softness over her waist. 'I'm not feeling very fatherly at the moment,' he confided, shifting to bring her closer. 'Oh, darling! A man can only take so much of this torture! I want to take you in my arms and seduce you, make love to you.'

Her fingers spread out on his chest, trying to feel him through the thickness of his jacket. She smiled as she felt his reaction to her touch. 'Do you?'

'You witch!' He caught her chin between his fingers, tipping her face upwards for his kiss. 'You're the magic princess,' he told her, brushing her lips gently with his, touching his tongue to the inner edge of her upper lip. 'I'm afraid if I touch you, you'll disappear like Cinderella.'

'I'm scared too,' she admitted, her lips parting for his searching tongue. 'When I met you at the airport, I thought—I thought you'd just look at me and you'd know.'

Lyle grasped her wrists, lifting them up along his chest until her hands curled at the back of his neck.

His hands moved from her wrists to cup her face for his kiss. He kissed her lightly, softly, then drew back a little to watch as his fingers slid back down to explore the contours of her neck, the gentle swelling that started just below her shoulders in the front.

'Shh,' he ordered her. Her eyes widened and lost focus as his fingers found the peaks of her breasts through the stiff fabric. 'Do you like that?' he asked, his eyes taking the answer from hers. 'Kiss me, honey.'

Her lips lifted, parted, touched his. Her fingers curled in his hair as the kiss began. He was going to wait, to let her kiss deepen, let her set the pace. Then her fingers felt along the tensed muscles of his neck, the fingertips of one small feminine hand coming to rest on the soft, sensitive skin of his throat.

His lips plundered the soft invitation of her mouth. He found he could draw a groan from her throat with the touch of his tongue on her inner lips. She shifted and he held her with one arm, his other hand exploring the wonderful feel of her, settling on her thigh as she moved her leg restlessly against him.

The leg muscles under his fingers tensed as he explored. Her hand traced his throat to the barrier of his shirt. He drew her close, his heart thundering, his hands pushing the cotton skirt away, so that his fingers could feel the heat of her outer thigh.

Then he found the buttons of her shirt, pushed the fabric back and looked down at the thrust of her breasts against her bra. It was a sexy, lacy wisp of fabric, pushing up her rounded white breasts for his eyes. He touched the upper skin gently, feeling the roughness of his hands against her softness, stroking, his own passion surging in his thighs when she groaned and writhed in his arms. He bent down to the softness, probed the lace with his lips and took a rigid nipple in his teeth through the lace.

Gentle with his teeth, his heart thundering. George gasped and twisted, pulling against him and arousing herself even more. He slipped his hands under her shirt at the back, his fingers spreading, holding her as she twisted.

George. Wild and wanton in his arms. He pulled the softness close, felt her straining against him. Her fingers pushed at his jacket. He raised his head and found her lips seeking, taking his with a warm, open passion as her body twisted and tormented his with its closeness.

He pulled her down with him, on to the carpeted floor where he could lay her, lean over her and bury his face in the warm curves, probe the fullness of her uplifted breasts. He felt her fingers at his collar and he pulled his tie off with a rough, impatient jerk.

'Lyle...' She was spinning, grateful when he laid her down on the floor because she was trembling with weakness and need. His hands, his lips. She wanted him, needed him to—oh, God! Could anyone feel like this and live?

Her fingers were fumbling, blind, trying to get closer, past his jacket and the silk of his shirt. Her breasts were swollen against the restraint of her bra, his lips teasing through the fabric.

His hands were hot under her breasts, his tongue tracing fire on the upper surface. 'Tell me what you want,' he whispered, his hands spreading down over her trembling midriff.

She lifted swollen eyelids to him. Her breath hurt her chest. Pulses thundering everywhere, a hot, heavy pulse beating at the centre of her. She'd never have dreamed she could ask, but she spread her fingers through the hairs of his chest, felt his heart slamming against it, saw his face filled with a desperate need.

'You,' she whispered. 'Lyle, make love to me.' His hands tightened, squeezing her breasts and she gasped, 'I want to feel you against me, naked.'

He lifted himself away from her and she said painfully, 'Please don't stop, whatever you do. Lyle, I—I went to the doctor. I'm—ready for you.'

His palm rubbed gently along her midriff, up over her bra. He watched her eyes. 'I know you're ready for me,' he said softly. 'Lie still, darling. You're going to need me the way I need you.'

He took her hands away from his chest. She could almost see herself reflected in his eyes. Lying below him, her shirt parted over swollen breasts, her full skirt strewn around her legs. He found the front fastening of her bra and let her breasts spring free, watching and claiming them with large palms, bending his lips to one hard peak, then the other. His tongue stroked at her rigid arousal, sending her body writhing.

He lowered himself over her, finding her lips again, pulling her softness against the bare chest exposed by his open shirt. His fingers sought the fastening to her skirt.

'It's a wrap-around,' she gasped, moving to give him access to the belt that anchored the skirt.

The skirt was gone, and his hands were drawing the clinging tights down along her legs. Then there was nothing to make a barrier for his hands or his lips as he explored her white softness, finding all the ways that he could bring a moan of desire to her lips.

When she could bear no more, she found her hands gripping his chest, digging into the muscles. She explored the hard ridges that led to his abdomen, followed a sprinkling of hair down to the buckle of his belt where it had pushed hard into her own body. Then her fingers fumbled, and his were there to help her.

He gasped as her fingers explored farther, groaning, 'George, if you—oh, darling...' He shifted, pulling her under him, his hard bare thigh sliding between her legs.

Then he was over her and she was open, waiting for him, her hands gripping him suddenly, urgently, pulling him into her as he thrust down, taking her, making her his in a spinning explosion that took them both tumbling into a wild, urgent carousel.

Sound roaring in her ears, hands and lips and skin, his rigid maleness possessing her void. The tension built and built, blood pounding through her veins. Coiled like a spring, she felt herself pushed past the point of no return, heard her voice crying out his name, her fingers clutching. Then she lost everything. There was a long, shuddering explosion, a spasm that flooded over her, then slowly receded, leaving her weak and spent, tangled in his arms...

Some time later, when she could open her eyes, George let herself enjoy looking at the smooth exhaustion of Lyle's face, his lowered eyelids, the tumble of unruly hair across his forehead, the faint sheen of perspiration on his skin.

His eyes opened, deep blue staring into hers. Her fingers touched his lips as he said softly, 'That was something, wasn't it?'

Her lips curved. She saw his eyes dropping, enjoying the curve of her breasts. 'It was incredible,' she found herself saying.

His hand possessed her breast, cupping it without passion. 'Maybe we could do it again some time?' His thumb found a softened nipple, and stroked it gently to rigid attention.

'Now?' she asked, gasping from a fresh surge of desire.

'Yes, now,' he agreed, bending to her lips again, drugging her with a deep kiss. 'I need you again,' he whispered against her lips.

Outside, the wail of a siren grew and came closer. He stiffened, hearing it.

'The hospital,' she said.

'Visiting hours,' he reminded them both. 'Robin.' He drew his lips back, his hands still telling her of his desire. He saw her face, the vulnerable parting of her lips. He half smiled, asking, 'Will you keep it warm for me? For later?'

'Later,' she agreed, letting her hand caress the hard core of his need.

'George, you devil!' His breath was hot in her ear, his hands pulling her back. She slipped away, came to her feet, standing over him, looking down.

Her breath quickened as he took in the wonderful sight of her standing in front of him. Her hands settled on her hips, her breasts thrust out slightly as she taunted softly, 'I wouldn't want you to forget.'

'George...' He stood up, moved towards her. She stepped back, picking up her clothes from the floor in a smooth motion.

'Will you stay with me tonight?' he asked hoarsely.

'Yes.' Her clothes were in her hands, half-covering the warm flush of her skin. 'I love you, Lyle.'

He said quickly, 'George, you don't have to say that. We'll take it easy. I don't want you to feel trapped, or——'

'I don't want to take it easy.' She took a deep breath, said on a rush, 'I want you. I want—oh, Lyle! I hope you really meant it when you said you loved me, because otherwise I'm making a big fool of myself. I—but I don't care. Oh, damn! I don't know how to say any of this! But you fished me out of the water. I crashed on your island, and you took me in.' She smiled, but her eyes were suddenly vulnerable. She whispered, 'You wouldn't cast me off, would you? You wouldn't do that to a stray lady?'

He moved towards her. She stepped back nervously.

'George, stop running away long enough for me to catch you!'

He caught her in his arms, clothes and all. 'I love you! God! You've known that for ages. I love you and I want every bit of you that you can give. Today and tomorrow and for ever!' He buried his face in her soft throat, groaned, 'Now, please, lady! Get your clothes on before I forget I've got a daughter waiting for us to visit!' He laughed, 'I've got a very special present for her—you!'

CHAPTER TEN

ROBIN was propped up on pillows, the back of the bed elevated to help her sit. One leg was thick under the blankets, wrapped in bandages.

'How are you doing, honey?' Lyle bent to kiss her cheek.

She half smiled. Her eyes were unfocused, groggy from the painkilling drugs that had been administered. 'The doctor said my leg's good as new,' she mumbled. 'Is George here? I want to tell George.'

'I'm here.' George moved to let Robin see her without twisting her neck. 'And I heard. It's wonderful news, love.' She took her hand and felt the girl's fingers curl in hers.

Robin's eyes drooped. Her voice was a bit muffled. 'Do you think you would like to marry my daddy?' She gestured vaguely to the other side of the room, where a red-headed girl was busily devouring a comic book. 'Marg'ret had her mummy die, and her daddy married a new one.' She opened her eyes. 'My daddy's pretty nice.'

'Yes, he is.' George found she had a lump in her throat.

'Do you think it's a good idea?' the girl asked anxiously, but her eyes closed before she could hear the answer.

Lyle took George's hand and gently freed it from his daughter's. He said softly, 'I think it's a good idea. I've been trying to tell you that for quite a while.'

She turned to face him. 'You never actually asked me. If you want a woman to marry you, you're supposed to ask.'

185

He gripped her upper arms, bringing her closer. She could feel his breath on her face. 'You made it pretty clear that you didn't want— George, will you marry me?' He took a deep breath, then said quickly, 'Damn it, woman! Before you answer, I warn you that I'm not taking no for an answer that easily. I vowed to myself that I wouldn't push you, but you admitted that you love me, and——'

'Yes,' she said, her hands spreading against his chest.

'——there's got to be a way that it will work. I——'

'Yes,' she said again.

'Yes?' His hands tightened painfully on her arms. 'George, you—I know you don't think—don't want to live on a lighthouse. If we——'

'It doesn't matter.' She raised herself up on her tiptoes, brushing her lips against his in a fleeting caress. 'I don't care. I want to marry you. I want to be your wife and Robin's mother and —and I want you to give me a baby. You keep trying to protect me from getting pregnant. But I'm thirty, and if I'm going to have a baby I should——'

'George, I love you.' He silenced the words coming from her lips. She snuggled closer against him. He said, 'About the lighthouse——'

She put her fingers on his lips, saying, 'I don't care. If it's what you want, I'll try it. I thought it mattered. When I left your island, I realised pretty soon that I loved you, but I didn't think I could live there. That's why I thought it would be good if Jenny and Jake got interested in a documentary.'

'To give me more choices, you said?'

'So you could leave the lighthouse. If you wanted.' She couldn't read the expression in his eyes.

'You mean, if I wanted you?' He pushed her away a little, to see her face better.

She frowned. 'You don't like that, do you? Yes, that's what I was thinking. That I loved you, but I couldn't live there. That I didn't think it was good for you or for Robin to stay away from the rest of the world for too long—or for me. I thought—I'm sorry, but that's what I thought.'

He caught her back to him. She realised then that he was laughing, his voice husky against her lips. 'Why didn't you tell me what you were thinking, you stubborn woman?' He parted her lips with his, tasting deeply of her sweetness. 'I was going mad, thinking you were trying to straighten out my life for some damned altruistic motive. Can you stand one summer?'

'One summer of what?'

He kissed the corner of her mouth, her nose, the soft skin of her eyelids. 'Green Island. My mother wants Robin to visit her for a while. I had to concede that it would be a good idea, because she's close to a physiotherapy clinic there, and Robin seemed to enjoy being there. She was making friends with a couple of sisters that lived next door. You could come back with us, and meet my mother, and marry me.' His lips claimed hers for another long kiss.

She said yes, but he didn't seem to hear. He went on, 'We could leave Robin with my mother for a while, go back to Green Island for a couple of months. We'd have the plane, and—well, we might spend a lot of time in the bedroom, so you wouldn't see too much of the island.'

She giggled. 'Just the bedroom ceiling?'

'And me. I could give my notice. We might just have enough time on the island to let Jenny and Jake do that documentary.'

She pushed back from him. 'Lyle, I don't think I was right to try to get you off the lighthouse. I don't want to pressure you, and——'

'I've been working towards it for the last couple of years, honey. I've been putting all my extra money into a helicopter company on Vancouver Island. It's a small company, but I've got enough in it now that I could leave and we could move down there. The fellow I'd be partners with is a single man. He'd take the overnight jobs and I could stay close to home. It's not far from my parents' place. You'd like them, and they'd love you. We could find a small place in the country, room to let the kids run. We——'

'Lyle?'

He fell silent, although his hands couldn't stop their gentle caresses, drawing her closer as they spread on her back.

'Kiss me?' she asked huskily.

He laughed, but he was already moving closer. 'There's a very interested young girl watching from the other side of the room,' he warned her.

She glanced back and saw Robin's new friend Marg'ret watching them with an eager smile.

She turned back and slipped her arms around Lyle's neck. She whispered, 'All I asked for is a kiss. The rest is for later. When we're alone.'

He kissed her.

Then he took her away, where they could be alone.

Harlequin Presents

Coming Next Month

1119 COMPARATIVE STRANGERS Sara Craven
Nigel's betrayal had shattered Amanda's dreams of their happy life together.
She doesn't know where to turn until Malory, Nigel's elder brother, takes
charge. He's a virtual stranger to her, yet she finds herself agreeing to
marry him!

1120 LOVE IN A MIST Sandra Field
A disastrous early marriage had brought Sally a small daughter she adored but
left her wary about love and commitment. It was ironic that trying to make a
new start on a holiday on St. Pierre she should meet attractive Luke Sheridan.
He felt exactly the same way she did....

1121 HEART OF THE HAWK Sandra Marton
As a step-aunt with skimpy earnings, Rachel has no legal chance of keeping her
nephew when his wealthy father comes to claim him. She discovers why David
Griffin is called The Hawk—and begins to realize the complications facing her.

1122 TRIAL OF INNOCENCE Anne Mather
Throughout her marriage to Stephen Morley, Robyn kept her guilty secret.
And she has no intention of revealing the truth now—even though Stephen is
dead and his brother, Jared, is asking questions that demand answers!

1123 TOO MUCH TO LOSE Susanne McCarthy
Jessica doesn't deserve her reputation as a scarlet woman, but finds it
impossible to set the record straight. Not that she cares what people think,
especially Sam Ryder. She needs him to save her business—that's the only
reason he's in her life.

1124 TAKE THIS WOMAN Lilian Peake
Kirsten is surprised when she inherits her late employer's country mansion.
She's even more surprised to find herself attracted to his great-nephew, Scott
Baird—especially when Scott wants to ruin all her plans and dreams.

1125 IMPOSSIBLE BARGAIN Patricia Wilson
Money is all that matters to Merissa—for the best of reasons. But Julian
Forrest doesn't know them and promptly jumps to all the wrong conclusions
about her. So why should he want her to pose as his fiancée?

1126 SHADOWS ON BALI Karen van der Zee
Nick Donovan broke Megan's heart two years ago when he plainly rejected her.
Now, meeting again, they're forced to work together on the same project in
Bali. And to Megan's disgust, Nick expects her to behave as if nothing had
happened!

Available in November wherever paperback books are sold, or through
Harlequin Reader Service:

In the U.S.
901 Fuhrmann Blvd.
P.O. Box 1397
Buffalo, N.Y. 14240-1397

In Canada
P.O. Box 603
Fort Erie, Ontario
L2A 5X3

Taylor House

by Leigh Anne Williams

Enter the lives of the Taylor women of
Greensdale, Massachusetts, a town where
tradition and family mean so much. A story of
family, home and love in a New England village.

Don't miss the Taylor House trilogy, starting next
month in Harlequin American Romance with
#265 *Katherine's Dream*, in October 1988, and
followed by #269 *Lydia's Hope* and
#273 *Clarissa's Wish* in November and
December of 1988.

One house . . . two sisters . . .
three generations

Harlequin Superromance

**Here are the longer, more involving stories you
have been waiting for...Superromance.**

Modern, believable novels of love, full of the complex
joys and heartaches of real people.

Intriguing conflicts based on today's constantly
changing life-styles.

Four new titles every month.
Available wherever paperbacks are sold.

SUPER-1

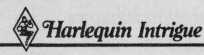